W9-BJZ-537

DATE DUE		
OCT 0 8 2021		
WITHDRAWN		

THE PERFECT
LOVE SONG

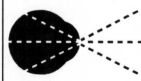

This Large Print Book carries the
Seal of Approval of N.A.V.H.

THE PERFECT LOVE SONG

A CHRISTMAS STORY

PATTI CALLAHAN HENRY

THORNDIKE PRESS
A part of Gale, a Cengage Company

GALE
A Cengage Company

**LIBRARY OF CONGRESS CIP DATA ON FILE.
CATALOGUING IN PUBLICATION FOR THIS BOOK
IS AVAILABLE FROM THE LIBRARY OF CONGRESS**

ISBN-13: 978-1-4328-7076-8 (hardcover alk. paper)

Published in 2019 by arrangement with Thomas Nelson, Inc., a division
of HarperCollins Christian Publishing, Inc.

Printed in Mexico
1 2 3 4 5 6 7 23 22 21 20 19

May stillness be upon your thoughts
and silence upon your tongue!
For I tell you a tale that was told at the
beginning . . .
the one story worth the telling.
— A TRADITIONAL IRISH
STORYTELLER'S OPENING

1

The truth inside the story is what the
storyteller aims for.
— MAEVE MAHONEY TO KARA LARSON

The Unknown Souls lived for the music,
for the notes and the lyrics and the rarefied
moment when it all came together in something greater than the sum of its parts,
greater than the writer and the instrument
and the voice. They waited through the
other songs — all lovely and rough and
sweet and melancholic — through the end-
less gigs, because they believed in the songs,
and the stories hidden inside. They believed
in the power of music and lyric to change a
life. Little did they know that their belief
would soon be fulfilled, that their hope in
things unseen would be as evident as the
stages on which they stood.

The story of the ballad that changed their
lives began on an early and dusky Thanks-

giving morning as the band's battered tour bus pulled into Seaboro, South Carolina, a small town waking up to the hanging of garlands, wreaths, and bows for the approaching holidays. The gas lanterns spilled golden light onto the damp streets and holiday lights were being strung from every storefront, but this sign of holiday arrival meant little to the bedraggled group half-asleep in varied positions on the threadbare seats. It was just another day, just another road trip for the band members. This time, however, the port of call was an exception for Jack and Jimmy. The brothers arrived in their childhood hometown, not for a concert, but to see their loves.

On a band's tour bus, holidays didn't mean so much. Time slipped by during the nights they forgot to sleep and the days of highway ribbon unfurling beneath the wheels. But that day Jimmy Sullivan did know what day it was — Thanksgiving morning.

He was the only one awake, his head lolling against the grimy window, aching with the kind of depletion that isn't easily cured with Tylenol and Gatorade. His brother, Jack, was asleep in the back seat. Ole Bud, the driver, had done his duty, driving through the night.

Jimmy and Jack Sullivan founded the band ten years ago, and the five of them had been together ever since. Jimmy played the acoustic guitar and Jack the bass guitar. Their duo of voices blended in most of the songs and yet each had his own style when singing alone. They wrote and traveled together, as bonded, loving, and argumentative as any two brothers could be. Then there was Harry, the drummer; Isabelle, the backup singer; and Luke, the band manager and keyboard player, each as close as family.

Jimmy opened the bus window, slamming it down with a few hammers of his hand, and noticed the palms bent low in submission, took in the sweet smells of earth, sea, and salt. It was a balmy coastal morning, the air infused with the rain of the past two days. He inhaled the aroma of childhood, then closed his eyes to all the good and bad of the visceral memories that assaulted him each time he believed he'd overcome the past.

Within minutes, the bus lurched onto the side of the road in front of a small one-story brick house hidden behind a forest of magnolia and oak. Above, the tree's branches wove themselves into a crochet pattern of green netting. Jack awoke as Bud slammed into park and called out, "Destination reached."

Jack stood and walked toward the front of the bus, cranking his neck left and right, rubbing at his eyes until he reached Jimmy. "We're here."

Under normal conditions, Jimmy wouldn't have wanted to stay for this gathering, no matter how much his brother prodded; he'd rather hang out with the band or fiddle with his guitar and write a song. He wasn't much on domestic events, even if the family belonged to his brother's fiancée, Kara, who was their childhood next-door neighbor. But there was one thing that could change a man's mind — a woman. And the woman who made Jimmy want to celebrate the holidays, Charlotte Carrington, was waiting inside that house on the coastal river.

With his holiday memories about as sordid as they come, he was usually as bah humbug as Ebenezer, but lately Jimmy felt like he was living in a sappy country song. He'd known Charlotte for a few years as a child and they'd reconnected months ago. At first, he'd denied this blooming love to his brother and anyone who would listen. But no one believed him, because love like that was obvious to everyone within a heartbeat's distance.

Isabelle made her way to the front of the

bus, gathering her things on the way. "We'll take off and leave y'all alone today." Her smoky voice was somehow both tough and tender.

"Nope," Jack said. "You're staying. We're family, and it's Thanksgiving." A band counted as family, and they all knew it. For a few of them it was the only family they cared about.

Jimmy stood, wrapping his left arm around Isabelle with a squeeze as Bud opened the bus with the hiss of the powered doors. Humid air poured in, and Jimmy squinted into the sunlight. Porter Larson, Kara's dad, stood in his pressed khakis and blue button-down, waiting with a wide smile and a wave. Jack jumped first from the bus, and Porter hugged him.

Now, that was a Thanksgiving miracle, because Mr. Larson had been none too keen on Kara breaking up with Mr. Hotshot Golfer to connect with an old neighbor who was now in a country-singing band. But Porter's smile and hug sang of a changed spirit. After he'd seen Jack's deep love for Kara, and Kara's happiness at having Jack back in her life, how could Porter deny his daughter the true joy of knowing the partnership and intimacy he'd had with his own wife, a woman he still mourned every day?

11

"Happy Thanksgiving," Porter hollered into the bus as Jimmy climbed out and stepped onto the damp grass. "Ready to join us for the day?"

One by one the group descended from the bus, wiping at their eyes and stretching. Isabelle answered, "Happy Thanksgiving to you, Mr. Larson, but I think we're headed to the beach for the afternoon. We have a concert in Nashville tomorrow, so —"

"Oh no you don't," Porter said. "You're coming to spend the day with us."

Luke, in his Unknown Souls black T-shirt and wrinkled sweatpants, stepped forward. "We're fine, Mr. Larson. We just need to find a place to clean up and shower and then we'll be out of your hair. You've got your hands full with the Sullivan boys here."

"Please," Porter said. "We'd love it, and we have plenty of food. Kara and Charlotte have been cooking for days. The kayaks are in the river. The hammock is strung up. The turkey is in the oven, and the beer is on ice."

The band members glanced at one another.

Harry's long brown hair hung loose and tangled, and he was holding drumsticks in his hand, as he always did. "Now there's a seductive invitation." He nudged Isabelle. "And I'm betting Kara's turkey is better than a sub sandwich."

"Then it's decided." Mr. Larson waved his hand toward the house. "Now, follow me."

The bus engine coughed and revved as Bud drove off to visit a friend on the other side of town while Jimmy, Jack, Harry, Luke, and Isabelle trailed behind Kara's dad like a group of misfit toys needing showers and naps.

The house was bright and warm as they entered. The smells of cinnamon and roast turkey filled Jimmy with a longing for things both lost and never experienced. He scanned the room for the reason he had agreed to this stop along the tour route — and there she was: Charlotte, with her long blond curls catching the firelight, hugging Jack and then Luke and Harry. Jimmy marveled at the light that seemed to radiate from her. As if his stare kissed her cheek, she turned and looked at him, her smile widening. She came to him and threw her arms around his neck.

In the middle of the room they held each other, and for a brief moment the world faded. Jimmy took her face in his hands and kissed her. "I missed you, sweet you."

"You too." She kissed him again.

"When I see you," he said, "the world

lights up. I've never seen anything like it. How did I ever deserve this?"

She laughed, that beautiful sound that could drop the chains from any man's locked-up heart. "So unexpected," he said and shook his head.

"Isn't that the best sort? The unexpected?" She turned her attention back to the room. When she did this — when she turned her light from him to others — he felt a flash of something akin to jealousy. But it faded quickly.

Then the sounds of family grew louder; Kara's sister and her husband, Deidre and Bill, walked through the front door in matching sweatshirts adorned with a turkey, juggling plastic containers of food and a case of wine. Kara's brother, Brian, followed. His fishing shirt and shorts were as muddy as if he'd just climbed out of the river. He held up a cooler labeled "Fresh Shrimp."

Charlotte came and took it from him and kissed his cheek. "You catch 'em, I'll cook 'em."

The house filled with the cacophony of family, of laughter and private jokes. The band crowded the living room, appearing misplaced on the prissy antique furniture of Mr. Larson's living room, which looked exactly the same as it had the day his wife, Margarite, passed away twenty years ago.

Jimmy took it all in. While the others showered and changed and he waited his turn, he soaked up the atmosphere. This, he imagined, if their dad hadn't been a fall-down drunk, if he'd been a decent man . . . this was what their life would have been like. Shrimp from the river behind the house. Laughter and warmth starting the holidays.

Jimmy avoided looking out the window at the two-story A-frame next door. He and Jack had lived in that house until he was sixteen and Jack was twelve. Until that fateful Christmas morning when their mother packed up the station wagon with everything they could fit into it, drove to Texas without the gifts that had been under the tree, and hadn't stopped for anything but gas, drinks, and packaged food from convenience stores off the highway. She drank Mountain Dew to stay awake, and the radio blared with whatever station came in along the bleak highway.

Jimmy shook off the memory and returned his attention to the living room.

Green damask curtains fell to the floor where Isabelle, who had exchanged her usual tattered jeans for a black dress, sat primly on a cushion, her long black hair, still wet from her shower, dripping onto her shoulders. She began to tell stories, ones about Jimmy and his antics on the road.

She was good at this, and everyone laughed as she told the tale about Jimmy hiring a girl to run up onstage and dance around Jack, trying to rope him with a lasso as he sang the Toby Keith song "Should've Been a Cowboy."

Jack entered the room in the midst of the telling, running his hands through his wet hair. "I'm telling you, I almost killed him, but what would we do without Jimmy's jokes on tour? I think sometimes they save us from insanity, even when we beg him to stop."

The voices and warm food, the wine and deep laughter filled the room. Charlotte's mother, Rosie, appeared just in time for dinner bearing a dessert tray covered in tinfoil that looked too heavy to carry. Charlotte's dad had passed only five years ago, and Rosie still seemed to turn to look for him whenever she walked in a room.

Sometimes Thanksgiving Day is all it should be in a family and in a home. That day inside the Larson home was one of those. In the simple and complicated way of love, relationships were stitched together over food, twinkling lights, bad jokes, and melancholy memories. They talked about Maeve Mahoney, the Irishwoman Kara believed had brought her back to Jack. They spoke of Kara's mother, Margarite, and how both Margarite and Maeve seemed to be present in all that was said and done that day. They remembered Charlotte's dad and his loud jokes that were funny only in the way they weren't funny at all, and how he would laugh so heartily at his telling that everyone just joined in. They spoke of Jack and Jimmy's sweet mother, Andrea, now in California.

Jimmy couldn't tear his gaze from Charlotte, with her laugh, her tender touch, and her gentle words. Families had never been a safe place for Jimmy, and he'd believed they never would be, like growing up in a war-torn country and then believing that all lands were embattled. But he was beginning to relax into the rhythm of a new place where Charlotte inhabited not just the Lowcountry but also his country.

The tangled memories of the house next door often left Jimmy dizzy. How should he feel about a place where he had lived with a mother as loving as his, a place where he had grown up, in this quaint, coastal town, and yet a place where an abusive and drunk dad hung like a poisonous cloud over their lives?

Only a woman like Charlotte could get him to return.

As the friends sat down on the back screened-in porch at the end of Thanksgiving Day, the cool evening breezes flowing off the river and twilight flirting with the water, tossing sparkling light across its basin, the reminiscing began.

It was Harry who asked, yawning from the porch swing where he'd just awoken from his second nap, "Someone please tell me how this man here" — he thumped the back of Jack's head with his thumb — "came to fall for this gorgeous creature." He pointed at Kara. "Or should I say, tell me how she fell for him. It all seems quite unlikely."

Charlotte spoke first, snuggling closer to Jimmy on the porch's wicker couch. "Kara and Jack's love story has been told before, but it is so beautiful that I love to tell it again and again."

Kara held out her hands, palms up, as if offering the story to the room. "Charlotte tells it best, and I usually get too emotional anyway." She lifted her chin to her friend. "Will you?"

"Go on then," Luke said and popped open

18

a beer. "Spill it."

"You see . . ." Charlotte glanced around and then continued. "Jack and Kara were childhood sweethearts, but Jack and Jimmy moved away when Jack was only twelve." She grinned and leaned forward, now in her best storytelling mode. "Now, you can split a boy and girl apart, but here's what you can't do — take the love. No, sir. You just can't. Love moves the same way blood does — running and thrumming through every cell and unseen thing that makes us who we are."

"Good Lord, woman." Harry laughed. "Are you writing a song or telling a story?"

"Is there a difference?" she asked and tossed a wadded-up napkin at him that landed on the white painted floor.

"Point well taken. Go on."

Charlotte did go on, and she told the story of Kara and Jack, about how they found each other.

Their rekindled romance had begun in May of the previous year, when Kara was engaged to the wrong man. Not a bad man. Just wrong for her. Kara had lost her mother when she was nine years old, and her daddy was a strict man who just wanted his daughter to be happy and thought that her famous pro-golf fiancé was the best thing for her.

19

She wanted to please her daddy. Who doesn't? This is built into the human soul.

Kara was working as a director for the PGA Tour, not only a grand job in her father's eyes but also a vocation that allowed her to meet Peyton Ellers, who was a star on the PGA Tour. Peyton was all those things a girl like Kara, a good girl trying to do all the right things at the right time, would have looked for and loved. And sometimes when everything looks just right we think it is just right, when it merely appears that way.

About this time a woman named Maeve Mahoney from Galway, Ireland, entered Kara's very perfect life. Well, to be precise, Kara entered Maeve's life when Kara walked through the front doors of the Verandah Nursing Home and into Maeve's room, stating, "I'm here to spend some time with you."

Kara didn't mind coming to the nursing home; these visits were volunteer hours for the Junior League, and although she'd been "assigned" those hours, she entered Maeve's room with a sense of expectancy. When Kara found the woman asleep, she began to flip through her bridal magazines. Maeve awoke and watched the young woman, who seemed both harried and preoccupied, and in a melodic Irish voice, she launched into a story about true love.

Kara tolerated this woman's ramblings at first, believing that Maeve was a bit of crazy and had confused life, love, Ireland, and Seaboro into a mishmash of memories. She spoke endlessly about Galway Bay and how its waters connected her to the waters of South Carolina. But after a while, over the course of Kara's visits, it became evident that Maeve was telling a love story, one that sounded a lot like the tale of the Claddagh ring, a story clouded in myth with a little blarney thrown in for good measure, which Kara had once read in a child's book about the Emerald Isle.

Kara remembered that the Claddagh ring was a common symbol — two hands circling a crowned heart — worn by lovers and friends all over the world. A symbol of love and fidelity. The legend of the ring went something like this: There was a man from Claddagh, Ireland, named Richard Joyce. In the seventeenth century, he left the woman he loved and sailed to the West Indies for a job, but alas, on the way, he was kidnapped by Moorish pirates and sold into slavery. Eventually he apprenticed to a goldsmith in Algiers, where he crafted the first Claddagh ring of gold as a gift for the woman he loved back home, the woman he knew he would return to one day, the woman he believed would wait for him. When Richard was finally freed, he came home and discovered that his true love had waited; he gave her the ring, and they wed.

In broken fragments, Maeve told Kara of her own love, of her own Richard, a man Maeve had loved and lost. The tender story opened Kara's eyes to what she knew all along: she still loved Jack Sullivan, her childhood sweetheart and the man she never once stopped missing and thinking about. Still, Kara did not believe that Maeve's story was "real," as the details were far too close to the myth of the Claddagh ring.

Kara spent hours listening to Maeve, pondering the questions Maeve asked her, questions like, "If you knew the man you loved would return, would you wait for him?" and "Who was your first love?" As their bond grew deeper and Kara intuited that Maeve was as far from batty as the east is from the west, Kara listened with an intensity and openness about the man Maeve had loved, a man who'd set out on the dark seas and returned to find Maeve promised to another. Kara finally believed in both the true story and the myth, and the authenticity buried within the words of both.

When Maeve died, Kara realized she could no longer fill her heart with busyness and meaningless noise in a meager attempt to soothe her heart with cheap substitutes.

Who can tell the exact moment when a woman or man believes in something? Who can tell the exact moment when someone falls in love? Believing. Love. Same thing.

So, you see, both the myth of the Claddagh ring and Maeve's heartbreak story brought Jack and Kara back together. And sometimes, oh sometimes, it is powerful and reunited love that also changes everything else in the world.

Isabelle, now seeming to actually care about the love story, asked the question they'd all been thinking. "So that's how you two got together?" She pointed at Jimmy and Charlotte. "Because your best friend and brother fell in love?"

Charlotte squeezed Jimmy's hand. "Yes." She cleared her throat of emotion. "That night, when Kara rushed to find Jack at his concert and tell him the truth, to tell him that she loved him, Jimmy and I were there. After that, we found ourselves together at concerts and soon we realized we liked hanging out together, that we didn't want to be apart. That was what?" Charlotte paused. "A year ago?"

"Time flies," Isabelle said. "Seriously flies. How could all of this have happened only a year ago? Y'all sure make this cynical and calloused heart believe in happy endings."

Silence fell. Far off, an owl hooted and crickets began their evening serenade. Jack spoke first. "I've never heard the story told from beginning to end. It's amazing, isn't it?" He leaned over and kissed Kara.

She wiped her eyes with the back of her hand. "For a while there, I forgot it was about us."

"That's the thing," Charlotte said. "It wasn't just about you. It was about Maeve and myth and now . . . this." She kissed Jimmy's scratchy cheek.

Harry clapped his drumsticks together. "Dang, y'all, I feel like I just fell into a country song. Now I need someone to tell me something funny or the evening will be too sweet for me to handle." He scrunched his face and wrinkled his nose, and they all laughed, turning to one another to chat or just smile.

"Wait!" Luke called out. "Where is Maeve's family and what happened to her after she passed? I mean . . . did you keep in touch with the family after all of that?"

Kara closed her eyes to the memory. "Some of her family is here and some are in Ireland. She never knew I returned to Jack." She smiled. "When I understood I'd been making my life's choices based on what I thought I was *supposed* to do instead of being who I was meant to be — big difference — everything changed." She sighed and closed her eyes again. "I'm still trying to find a way to honor her in our wedding."

"We'll find something." Charlotte's voice fell softly into the sadness.

Isabelle stood, shook her hair, and stretched. "I think I'm done for the night." She nodded at Kara. "Thank you so much for the best Thanksgiving I've had in years."

Slowly, one by one, everyone ambled off to the kitchen or the couch where they could watch football playing on the TV or nap.

Only Jimmy and Charlotte remained on the porch, and she spoke to him softly. "We're all just too much sometimes, aren't we?"

"Yes," he said. "Sometimes."

"I'm sorry," she said. "I know holidays are . . . not your favorite."

"No, not my favorite," he said. "But you are."

She rested her head on his shoulder and sighed.

"Hold on," he said. "I'm going to get my guitar. Don't leave."

She smiled. "Where would I go when I know you're getting a guitar? Hurry."

He laughed and stepped away, returning quickly to sit next to her on the porch swing. "All this talk about how stories brought us together and how unexpected these love stories are and were . . . I thought . . ." He played a few chords and hummed, mumbling, "So unexpected, so divine, so unforeseen."

"Just think," she said. "We grew up in the same town and barely knew each other. You lived right there, and over those three years we crossed paths but barely paid each other any mind. I was much too young for you." She winked.

Jimmy again strummed the same melodic chord and sang a line about unexpected love, about the complete surprise of finding extraordinary where you thought only ordinary resided. Charlotte added a line about biding her time, about knowing that the right thing would come along, about waiting with faith for the unseen.

And within minutes, just like that, Jimmy and Charlotte had cowritten their very first song together. It was a ballad they believed was about the happenstance, fate, and legend that gave birth to the long-awaited love between them.

Jimmy quickly typed the lyrics into his phone notes, and Charlotte repeated her lines for him. When they were done, he looked at her with wonder. "How did you know how to do that?"

"Do what?"

"Write a song."

"I didn't write a song. I just told you some of my poetry lines." She turned away, blushing. "I mean, I never show my writing to anyone. I just scribble it for myself. But no one will ever hear this, so it's okay. It's just ours."

"You instinctually understand the rhythm and cadence of lyrics, Charlotte. Why didn't I know this about you?"

"It's just a poem. I've been writing them all my life. It's not something important like a song."

"But, my love," he said, "there are songs we never grow tired of — lyrics about going home, about love, about redemption, about brokenness and healing. And you hit all of that with just a few words. I know songs, and you just wrote one with me."

She nodded. "You make it sound like

music can save us."

"It can. It always has."

She smiled at Jimmy. "Well then, looks like I'm more than just another pretty face." She elbowed him and laughed.

He kissed her so gently. "You never cease to amaze me."

2

Your story, your life, and your journey all involve what came before you and what comes after — all hints of who you are.
— MAEVE MAHONEY TO KARA LARSON

Exhausted and sated, the band found their usual seats on the bus and dozed off as they headed toward Nashville. Isabelle moaned. "I should not have had that last piece of pumpkin pie."

Jimmy moved to the back seat and watched his childhood home fade from view. Although he'd been back to Seaboro a few times since Jack and Kara reunited, the last time he'd watched the house get smaller and smaller, he'd been in a wood-paneled station wagon with his sobbing mother driving away from their fall-down-drunk dad, with their belongings crammed in the trunk. He turned away from the view and the memory.

As the older brother, he'd always felt he should have been able to protect Jack and his mama from a drunk dad. Jimmy didn't like to use the word *dad,* but he didn't like to call him by his first name, Wagner, either, as if he knew the man, as if Jimmy was intimately connected with his dad enough to say his name out loud. Jimmy preferred not to talk about or think about his dad in any way, but how can a son do such forgetting?

When Jimmy and Jack finally escaped the grip of Mr. Sullivan's whiskey breath and callous hands, they'd also left Jack's childhood love, Kara, and the town of Seaboro behind.

As children they'd drowned out their parents fighting with the blaring music of the four-foot-tall speakers they set up in their shared bedroom. Hank Williams, George Jones, Merle Haggard, and Loretta Lynn filled the emptiness with their crooning, love, guitars, and heartbreak. Jimmy and Jack found that music muffled the sounds of anger but also filled the void that pain carved in their lives.

In a secondhand shop in downtown Seaboro that smelled like old gym clothes, Jimmy and Jack combined their saved quarters, lawn-mowing cash, and Christmas money to purchase a banged-up guitar. Once in Texas, a wide-open state where they grew up with their band and their songs, the brothers started their music-making in earnest. Jimmy and Jack grew up not only as brothers but also as each other's father, one taking the place when the other needed it the most.

Now, you'd think that they'd have been thrilled to have a drunken, beat-them-up dad out of their life, but in memory a dad is a dad, and a boy can miss the image of him more than he can miss the actual person. Music became the thing between the brothers that a father could have been: a bond, a teacher, a feeling of something meaningful and wholesome.

Together, Jimmy and Jack wrote music, played music, talked about music. At some point they began to live for the music. With their band, the Unknown Souls, they traveled through the southern United States to get their name out there, opening for acts like Vince Gill and Martina McBride. On this path, they found their way in the world. It was not the course most would take, but it was theirs. And until Jimmy met Charlotte, he believed the music would always be enough.

■ ■ ■ ■

Jimmy didn't love her the first time he met her. It wasn't that kind of story. Charlotte was merely his brother's girlfriend's best friend, like an extra in a movie or the minor character in a novel. Charlotte was full of smiles and laughter, a tender light in every corner of every room. This was the opposite of Jimmy — he was boisterous, loud, and jocular in a take-up-the-air-in-the-room kind of way. His light was more like a blinding lightning strike.

They'd seen each other again at a PGA Tour party that Kara had organized. She had hired the Unknown Souls to play for the championship award ceremony. The party conversation had been confusing to Jimmy. He knew nothing of the sport, didn't care about scores and putts and birdies.

Jack wasn't having a good night either. Kara had been preoccupied with her job and her then-fiancé (who had just lost the championship with one last putt). Jack and Kara had reconnected months before, and Jack had believed they were in love, and yet now here was Kara with her hotshot fiancé. Jack's heart was breaking, but he didn't want to face that fact and he was flat-out angry.

Jimmy tried to calm and soothe his brother, but Jack had been insistent on getting as far away from Kara as quickly as possible. They escaped the party like the police were after them, leaving no time to truly notice Charlotte — he said hello, smiled. The End. Or so he thought.

Now, Charlotte might not be the first person you notice at a party, but by the end of the night, she might be the only one you remember. And this is what happened to Jimmy. Charlotte crossed his mind in the same way as a nice sunset or laughter-filled party, a gentle but insistent memory.

Then months later, after Kara *finally* broke up with her fiancé and ran to find Jack and profess her love, Kara invited the brothers to her house for a cookout. At some point Jimmy found himself alone on the back porch with Charlotte. Mr. Larson had been grilling steaks, and the air was resonant with spices and charcoal.

From where they were standing, the white-shingled corner of Jimmy's childhood home was just barely visible through the trees.

Charlotte asked, "Is it odd to see your old house?"

"Yes," he said quietly. "I try not to think too much about it. Sometimes when I look at the house it seems like something out of a scrapbook, not really mine at all."

"I know," she said in a tender voice, almost like she was singing a lullaby to a tired child, and then turned and smiled at him.

When she did this, Jimmy felt something shift inside him, but he dismissed the feeling, thinking it was an odd emotion passing over him because of the house and all.

When he didn't smile in return, Charlotte put her hand over her mouth. "I'm sorry. I didn't mean to sound like a know-it-all. Kara has told me so many stories about you and Jack living there. She loved your mama, and she loved when y'all lived there. She told me about the time you rode your bike through the kitchen claiming the brakes didn't work and you needed to hit something soft, which I believe was the couch. She says hanging out at your house were some of her best childhood memories and that you made her laugh all the time. She says you were and are the funniest boy she's ever met."

Charlotte took a deep breath, and inside that small space — like the space between heartbeats — Jimmy let loose a laugh. Charlotte clearly thought he was making fun of her and turned away. He touched her arm. She looked over her shoulder. "I wasn't laughing at you," Jimmy said. "I was laughing with you."

"I was babbling. I do that sometimes. And I wasn't laughing," she said, "so technically you weren't laughing with me."

"No, I wasn't. But the way you talk sounds like you're laughing."

She smiled in that shy way.

Jimmy continued. "The brakes weren't broken. I just wanted to ride the bike through the house and the back door was open and . . . I did a wheelie over the top step, and then there I was, coasting through the kitchen and into the living room."

What Jimmy didn't tell her was that his dad then proceeded to smack him with a belt for getting mud on the living room carpet, for being an insolent boy who never had a lick of sense in his miserable head.

"Wow," Jimmy said, staring off toward the house. "The bike story. I'd forgotten."

"We do that, don't we?" she asked.

"Do what?"

"Forget the good parts because we are so busy forgetting the bad parts."

And that was the end of that. Jimmy's heart opened wide, as if an earthquake had moved the tectonic plates of his dismal childhood aside to let in Charlotte's love.

Mr. Larson had come out and called for

everyone to come inside for dinner. Charlotte left Jimmy standing there alone on the
porch, and he realized that his hands were
shaking and he had a desperate need to run
after her, after her joy.

We often don't know we've fallen in love
until we look back and say, "Ah, that was
the moment." And this is how it was for
Jimmy. He didn't know until he knew.

3

Your feet will bring you to where your
heart is.
— OLD IRISH PROVERB

Why, Charlotte wondered over and over as
she planned the decorations for the holidays, *is Christmas the most hectic time?* How
had what was once meant to be a slow and
calm remembrance of blessings, of the
Lord's birth, of joy and family, become a
chaotic jumble of parties, overspending,
family drama, and obligatory giving? Women
frantic to have better Christmas trees than
their neighbors — more lights, fancier
wreaths. As an interior designer, Charlotte
was experiencing one of her most profitable
weeks of the year, what with everyone wanting to outdo everyone else with the most
perfectly perfect Christmas decorations, as
if it were about the lights, garland, and yard
art.

Some people know right away what they are supposed to do in life; others wander and stumble until they find their vocation and say, "Wow, I should have been doing this all along." Charlotte was the first kind. She knew when she was five years old that all she wanted to do was make the spaces in and around her life more beautiful. She made her mama crazy moving furniture and repainting her room every six months. She scribbled poetry in notebooks she covered in flowers and peace signs. She colored her world both inside and outside. Charlotte knew this town, the houses, and the women better than anyone ever had. This was her gift.

Now, if anyone could have two opposite experiences with Christmas and family, it was Jimmy Sullivan and Charlotte Carrington. If you made a list and placed their lives one against the other, you would laugh and say that these two would never even meet as adults, much less talk, and absolutely not fall in love. But that is the pure beauty of love: it is what it is and it shows up when it wants to appear. Unseen and unpredictable. Just like their song — unexpected, but somehow long-awaited.

The morning after the band left for Nashville, Charlotte and Kara stood in the Larson kitchen baking their yearly Christmas cookies, which they put in tins and gave as gifts. This year they were also making shortbread in honor of Maeve Mahoney, adding it to the gift boxes they would give to friends and distribute at the nursing home. Although Kara had her own cottage, this kitchen was much better equipped for so much baking.

Kara leaned against the counter. "So how do you think you'll do with Jimmy on the road all month? It's awful, isn't it?" Kara's smile told of her conspiratorial gladness that Charlotte was in the same country music boat with her.

Charlotte wiped flour from her hands and picked up her mug of hot tea. "I don't know — I guess because I've never felt like this about anyone. It's awful *and* wonderful." She turned back to the cookies, plopped a candy silver ball onto the green icing of a Christmas tree cookie. "Missing someone you love isn't like any other emotion. That three-month break they took to write new songs spoiled me. It's harder now."

"I know," Kara said. "There's something comforting in knowing that the man you love is doing what he loves, but it still hurts."

Charlotte just nodded; she thought if she spoke, she'd cry. No one knew her like Kara

— they'd been best friends since second grade. Kara and Charlotte found each other during that time in life when Kara's mother's illness had left her scared and confused. Their common interest in art drew them together, although they didn't understand at that young age what had brought them together. They merely felt that their souls called out for the other in an immediate way.

Both made sense of life through an artistic expression of their hearts — Kara used her camera and Charlotte her design work and poetry. Charlotte displayed her interior design but hid her poetry; she always had and assumed she always would.

Other than their deep love for each other and for the Sullivan brothers, the friends had little in common. Kara was organized and precise where Charlotte was scattered and free-spirited. Kara's hair was a deep brown, straight and controlled; Charlotte's loose blond curls fell free and wild no matter what she tried to do with them. Kara's cottage was on the water, filled with white furniture and clean lines; Charlotte's one-bedroom house was hidden in a grove of palmetto trees and overflowed with swatches of fabric, paint chips, and poster boards toppling with ideas. Kara's books were in white-painted bookcases and lined up alphabetically by author; Charlotte's books were loosely arranged by color and style.

Sometimes friendships form in the long flow of days, like a river carving a new path through the land, and other friendships are wrought together like iron to iron in a single moment. The day of Kara's mother's funeral, the adults, engulfed in their own grief, had left the girls alone. Together they'd hidden under the branches and tangled roots of the old magnolia tree in the front yard. Curled into each other with ham sandwiches wrapped in flowered napkins, chocolate chip cookies melting in their pockets, they'd eaten, whispering stories of ghosts and angels, of where Margarite Larson was at that moment. Had she been able to talk to Jesus? After the devastation of chemotherapy, had all her hair grown back when they gave her a halo? They'd then fallen asleep to the lullaby of the wind, to the voices of adults wafting toward them but never fully reaching their ears.

When the darkness settled into the crevices of the yard, and when the day they buried Kara's mother finally ended, no one could find the best friends. Adults called their names, searched the neighbors' homes and yards. It was Jack who discovered them. It was Jack who knew where they'd gone and why. He slipped under the branches and woke them, knowing in that way that children know that the friends would not want anyone to see where they'd been. Together the three of them walked into the dark night, and Charlotte looked up to the brightest stars and said, "Do you think she can see us through those holes in the sky?"

"Those aren't holes, Charlotte," Kara said in a voice that was now more grown up than it had been the day before.

Charlotte stopped, grabbed her best friend's hand. "Tonight they can be holes in the sky, right?"

Kara stood for the longest time staring up into the sky and even past the sky, farther and deeper, until she returned her gaze to Charlotte and Jack. "Yes, well, yes, they can."

And together the three friends slipped quietly into the house, where their friendships had tied their first knots. From that moment on, Kara and Charlotte became as bonded as they were now in Kara's kitchen baking shortbread all these years later.

The holiday season sometimes fills us with unrealistic expectations, and the romantic visions of Jimmy sitting by the fire and drinking hot cocoa and talking about their future were in stark contrast to his quick departure in a beat-up bus. Charlotte wanted him there to decorate the tree, to hang the lights, to go to all the parties and events. But he wasn't. He couldn't be.

"I have so much to do, hopefully it will make time go faster. But for some reason I don't believe it will."

"Missing him will become part of every day, and it gets better. I promise."

Charlotte rolled dough onto the countertop. "I hope so. I really hope."

Yes, hope. What the holidays are all about.

The next day, Charlotte awoke at dawn, sat up in bed, and then walked across the hardwood floors to the window. She stared into the dusky morning where the neighbor's multicolored Christmas lights blinked like frantic eyes. She pictured Jimmy's bus moving down an unknown highway toward another gig. The morning noises outside were as comforting as they were familiar — birds and cars and the far-off sound of a train whistle. But then something new and unfamiliar entered — the crunch of tires on the gravel drive of her cedar-shake home. She turned sideways and spied a white car driven by a man, with another in the passenger seat. She quickly closed the curtains and shed her Christmas tree pajamas for a pair of jeans and a sweatshirt just as the doorbell rang.

When Charlotte peered through the peephole, curiosity turned to joy as she spied Jimmy Sullivan glancing left and right as though he was checking the surroundings, with Jack behind him. He ran his hand through his tousled hair and then glanced back to the door as Charlotte threw it open and flung her arms around his neck. "Jimmy!"

"Charlotte." He uttered her name with such tenderness.

Later that day, after Charlotte, Jimmy, Kara, and Jack had spent the day bundled up and riding around on Kara's dad's little boat through the estuaries and rivers of the Lowcountry, they gathered on Kara's porch. The boys had rented a car and driven all night to see their loves. There was a lull — a beautiful, syncopated beat between notes — and then they all began to talk about Kara and Jack's upcoming wedding. When and where and how and who — all the logistics that can turn a celebration into a chore, but Kara seemed to have other ideas.

Kara lifted her glass. "I know it's love that brought us together, but I might not have had the courage to go looking for Jack Sullivan if Maeve Mahoney hadn't reminded me how authentic love feels, if she hadn't asked me this one question: 'Would you wait for him if you knew, if you really knew he'd return to you?' When she asked me that, I knew that of course I'd wait a lifetime if he were really returning. So instead of waiting, what did I do? I went to find him. So, here's to Maeve Mahoney, her stories and her questions."

Overlapping voices shouted, "Hear, hear," as the glasses clanged together like heaven's wind chimes. Kara smiled. "Okay, so I think Jack and I have the best idea ever."

Jack took her hand and nodded for her to go ahead.

"Ireland. We want to get married in Ireland at Maeve's church — that chapel she always talked about in Claddagh. On Christmas Day."

Jack gazed at her with a grin and then glanced at Charlotte and Jimmy. "What do you think? I mean, I know it's last minute and we'd be scrambling for tickets, but we could do it. We don't have any gigs after the twenty-first."

And with that, the four of them were off and running with the plans, looking up flights and places to lodge in the Claddagh Village. As the night wound down, Jack brought up the song. "Jimmy tells me you helped him write his new song."

"I did?" Charlotte glanced at Jimmy and blushed. "All I did was give him a few lines."

"Well, that's what we call helping to write a song." Jack leaned back and laughed, his voice echoing across the room. "Sing it." He motioned to his brother. "Let Kara hear it!"

Jimmy picked up his guitar from the side of his chair and flung it over his shoulder, the leather strap with his name carved in red across his chest. As he sang, Charlotte grinned and wiped away the good kind of tears — ones of filling, not emptying. And for the first time in Jimmy's life, he believed that Christmas just might be different from any other holiday.

"That's incredible." Kara whispered the words as if afraid to scare the moment away. "The best thing you've ever done."

"Thanks. I think so too. All because of this one." Jimmy removed his guitar and set it next to Charlotte.

"What are you calling it?" Kara asked, slipping off her shoes and yawning as she moved closer to Jack.

" 'Unexpected.' "

"Ooh. I like it," Kara said. "It's gonna be a hit. Just you watch."

"Now what?" Charlotte asked, snuggling with Jimmy and feeling a wonder that they had made a song together, that by just giving him a few of her hidden lines of poetry they had created something beautiful. And it made her hope, and wonder . . . what else would they make together?

"What do you mean?" Jack stretched his legs across the ottoman.

"What gig do you have next?"

"Oh, tomorrow. Savannah."

"Ah! That's why you could leave the band for the day. Perfect. It's only an hour away."

They settled in with the contentedness of the evening, not knowing — how could they? — what would happen next with a song that had only been performed for three.

The Lowcountry coast during the holidays is one of the most tender and soul-stirring scenes in the world. The lights set against the hanging Spanish moss and whitewashed porches look like angels gathered to sing. That year December arrived in a warm, moist nuzzle. The fancy scarves and hats were of no use. Soon January would come in with a freeze that broke all records, but for now there was a reprieve.

Kara, Jack, Jimmy, and Charlotte drove to

Savannah on that December night. Charlotte drove her convertible because they believed the warm weather would allow them to put the top down, but after twenty minutes they decided it wasn't such a great idea. Charlotte drove the car to the side of the road, and Jimmy jumped out to pull the top up. Charlotte turned to the back seat and looked at Kara. "Remember that night your mama took us to see the lights in Savannah and she got a flat tire?"

Kara's eyes flashed. "Yes. Oh my gosh, yes. How do you remember that? We were, like, eight years old."

"And you wore a red taffeta dress with this huge green bow, and I wore this silly, scratchy wool dress my grandma made for me that Mama forced me to wear so Grandma could see the pictures. And it was just the three of us — me, you, and your mama."

Kara leaned forward in the seat, her left leg and arm draped over Jack's leg next to her. He didn't mind much. It seemed that every few minutes he was amazed again and again when realizing that this was his love. His Kara. Here was all he'd dreamed of during those years alone, during those years on the road. It was moments — simple moments like these — that stunned him the most. Like waking up in the middle of a dream and realizing you didn't wake up but that it was your life.

Kara said, "Mama got out to change the tire. Remember? And it was freezing and Christmas carols were on the radio."

"Yes." Charlotte raised her hands in the air. "And we were singing them really loudly. So loudly that your mama came back to the window and asked if we were crying. She thought we were upset."

Kara laughed in that pure, deep way, and she looked at Jack. "Yeah, you know that and love me anyway, right? You know I can't sing."

Jack smiled but didn't answer. He just wanted to bask in this memory he now relived with her.

Charlotte stared out the window. "And then that car stopped, and a man helped us. He was so old he didn't look like he could change his coat, much less a tire."

The top was up by now, and Jimmy climbed back into the car. Charlotte smiled at him. "We were just talking about a time when Mrs. Larson took us to Savannah to see the Christmas lights and we were stopped with a flat tire."

Jimmy smiled. "I remember her in this hazy way where I swear I see a halo around

49

her head. What a woman."

"Thanks, Jimmy." Kara looked up to the roof of the car for a moment and then back to Charlotte. "So that old man changed the tire. Mama told him she could do it — that she knew how. But she was wearing this long black skirt and silver high heels. It was cold out. I remember the heat pumping in the car. But the old man said there was no way he would allow her to change that tire on the left front side because she would be standing next to the traffic. He changed it in, like, one minute. And then he just drove off without letting us pay or thank him."

Charlotte nodded as she started the engine. "It was like an angel visitation. And then we had the best night in Savannah. We saw every light and every house and even went on that carriage ride after we'd begged and begged. We drank so much hot chocolate that you were sick on the way home." She exhaled into the memory.

They were all silent as they slipped into that place of remembrance.

What the four of them didn't know was that, yes, the essence of that story was true. Margarite Larson was a beautiful woman and they had a flat tire that night and spent a wonderful evening in Savannah, but the facts? Well, they were all mixed up. Kara wore silver. Charlotte didn't even own that scratchy dress yet (she received it for Christmas that year). What was true? The old man. What they didn't know was that he had been sent to help. Even in hindsight we don't always recognize all the unseen forces at work in our lives.

You see, stories change with every retelling. The people who speak the stories don't know they've changed the details a bit every time, but the story becomes a living, evolving thing. And here is the beautiful part — even if it sounds a little bit different each time it's told, the essence of the story remains.

That night the Unknown Souls were part of a "Holiday Jingle Jam" concert featuring six up-and-coming country artists. The Unknown Souls were plopped directly in the middle of the show, unfortunately in the exact same place as an intermission might be in a play or movie. Sadly, the audience used this as an opportunity to visit the concession stand and go to the filthy bathrooms. Those who did stay were talking or making out. Until Jimmy started singing his new song.

The hush that descended on the auditorium was almost holy. A quiet that caused people to hold their breath and open their eyes wide. It was a moment, well, many moments, when only the lyrics and music filled the place. A common man filling a common place with an uncommon song.

Kara and Charlotte were sitting backstage, sipping champagne and listening. They couldn't see the crowd, but when the quiet descended, they poked their heads out to make sure the stadium hadn't emptied.

"They love it," Kara whispered.

"They do, don't they?" Charlotte's voice was filled with wonder.

Kara put her arm around her best friend's shoulder and squeezed.

Jimmy bowed to the applause and returned backstage to Charlotte. "Hey, my beautiful girl, they seem to like you too." He kissed her in that soft way he had with her, as if she might break, as if she was the most fragile thing he'd ever held.

"I don't think it's me they like," Charlotte said. "It's you. Your song."

"Our song." He kissed her again and then held her face in both his hands.

"They have no idea about me." She laughed, slipped her fingers through his belt loops, and held fast.

The next moment a bald, stout, sweating man came running backstage. His name was

Milton Bartholomew, and he was in charge of these concerts. An expert in audience response. A man who knew when a song was destined to be a hit.

"Mr. Sullivan," he said to Jimmy in a loud voice, grabbing him by the forearm. "That song wasn't on the playlist."

Jimmy shook him loose. "Sorry, we substituted at the last minute."

Milton laughed so loud and long that his face turned red. "Whatcha apologizing for, son? It was brilliant. Truly brilliant. You wrote it about Christmas, didn't you? That's a Christmas song."

"No." Jimmy backed away from the boisterous man. "We wrote it." He squeezed Charlotte's hand. "And it's a love song."

"No, you wrote it about Christmas. It's the perfect Christmas song."

"Huh?" Jimmy stared back at Milton, thinking the man must have imbibed too much holiday cheer.

"The perfect Christmas song. All about unexpected and long-awaited love. All about letting that love into your heart to change the world." Milton's hands were flying all over the place as if he were throwing confetti.

Jack stepped forward now.

There are moments in life when the smallest action leads to the biggest changes. We rarely know when those moments are happening. But Jack felt it for his brother.

"You're right," Jack said and turned to his brother. "It's true. I didn't even realize it, but" — Jack turned to Milton — "you're right. It is the absolutely perfect Christmas song."

Just then country superstar Rusk Corbin, six foot six with his cowboy hat and boots on, walked by, searching for his guitar. He stopped to hear the end of the conversation. "What's the perfect Christmas song?"

Everyone stared at Rusk. Jimmy and Jack didn't answer, Charlotte and Kara were starstruck, and then Milton pulled out his cell phone.

Rusk tried again in that deep, baritone voice of his that made all hearts stop for a beat or two. "*What* is the perfect Christmas song?"

Milton covered the mouthpiece of his phone. "Aren't you on next?"

"I'm just looking for my backup guitar. Is someone going to answer me?"

Kara found her voice first. "Did you hear the last song?"

The country star shook his head. "Nope, I was in my dressing room."

"Well, Jimmy here" — Kara pulled Jimmy

forward — "is the lead singer for the Unknown Souls, and he wrote and sang the most magical song of the night."

She stopped, embarrassed and realizing that this star was part of the evening's songs. "Well," she said, smiling her cutest smile. "So far anyway."

"Can I hear it?" Rusk asked.

Milton stepped in now, placing his body between Kara and the star. "Ah, yes, you can. I'll get you a recording. But you go . . . You're on."

Rusk rolled his eyes and leaned toward Jimmy. "His bark is worse than his bite."

The foursome stared at him as he walked off with Milton and then they all burst into laughter. "The perfect Christmas song indeed," Jack said.

4

All of our lives we must choose between
what others define us to be and who we
are meant to be.
— MAEVE MAHONEY TO KARA LARSON

Marshside Mama's Restaurant and Bar in
Seaboro was crammed past the fire-code
regulations, but no one seemed to care,
what with the bluegrass band playing and
the space heaters keeping everything as
warm as mid-August. The crowd spilled
outside and onto the patio where Kara and
Charlotte sat at a round-top zinc table, leaning toward each other to discuss Kara's first
big paying photo shoot in the morning.
When Kara quit her job at the PGA Tour,
she'd fulfilled her dream of going to photography school and working in a studio.
Now, finally, she had her first solo job. Night
settled over the crowd, candles the only light
competing against the brilliant moon.

The haze of the previous night's Savannah concert had dissipated and the guys had boarded the band bus, leaving for the next gig. Now Kara and Charlotte sat sharing a plate of shrimp and grits.

"Have you told Jack yet?" Charlotte leaned closer, her voice pressing against the other voices and music.

"No, I want to tell him in person," Kara said. "He'll be thrilled. He knows what it means to be hired for something you love and would do anyway. Who else would get it?"

"Me. I'd get it," someone said from behind.

The girls recognized this voice immediately, yet they didn't turn; for a brief moment their eyes met and widened. Kara turned first. "Hello, Peyton," she said to her ex-fiancé.

"Hey, you." He hugged Kara, and she, in reflex, hugged him in return.

He stood there looking like the pictures Kara had once taken of him on the golf course — the epitome of the handsome athlete. His gaze moved to Charlotte, and his face hardened into a false smile that went only as far as the edge of his lips. "Hello, Charlotte."

"Hello, Peyton." She nodded at him but

didn't move from her seat.

The awkward silence that comes with a girl seeing her ex-fiancé for the first time since breaking off the engagement filled the air, a silence demanding that someone speak, but no one knew exactly what to say next.

"So, I wasn't eavesdropping," he said. "I was just walking past when I heard you say you got a big photography job." Peyton grabbed a bar stool from the adjacent table, dragged it over, and sat next to Kara, turning his back to Charlotte.

Kara scooted her stool closer to the other side so Charlotte wasn't blocked. "Yes, I was hired to shoot a family for a Christmas card."

"So, you really did it, huh? You really went back to photography school and left an entire career behind?"

Charlotte laughed, making a sound that was less like a laugh and more like a cough. "You're kidding me, right? She left a job to start a career."

He leaned back on his stool and stared at Charlotte with his blue eyes — eyes that held a light he could turn on and off at will. Charlotte stared into blue ice. "I guess that would depend on what you'd call a job or a career, wouldn't it?"

Kara held up her left hand. "Stop it, y'all."

Peyton saw it then: the engagement ring. He grabbed Kara's hand and pinched the diamond on either side. "Wow. You're engaged already? Less than a year since we broke up? I guess I was right . . ." He exhaled and stared off into the crowd.

"Right about what?"

"That it was someone else. That your little speech about not loving enough, or not knowing how to love me . . . It was a bunch of . . ." He didn't finish the sentence, but instead ran his hands through his hair, shaking his head.

"No, Peyton. That's not it. That's not entirely true." Kara paused and lowered her voice. "You know things weren't right between us."

"Yeah, and now I know why." He leaned forward and placed his hand over hers, covering the ring. "Can I ask you a question? I mean, we were in love, or at least I was in love, so can you be honest with me?"

Kara nodded; Charlotte rolled her eyes.

"Is it that guy from the band? The guy you hired for the PGA concert?"

"Yes," Kara said. "I've known him since childhood. He was once my best friend. It's not like I picked up some band guy and let him put a ring on my finger. I've loved Jack since I was a kid."

Peyton shook his head in a snarky kind of way. "Yeah, okay."

Kara pulled her hand out from under his. "Stop, okay? Let's not say hurtful or unkind things. It's good to see you. How are you?"

"I'm well. If you kept up with my career, you'd see how well."

"I know how you're doing out there on the course," Kara said. "I meant, how are *you*?"

"I'm okay. From the looks of it, this has been harder for me than it's been for you. It's taken me a while to get my feet back on the ground. I really thought we were *it* . . . you know? I really thought it was forever and if I just waited long enough, you'd realize it too, but here you are with a ring on your finger."

Charlotte stood now. "You know what? I think I'll go get us a couple drinks at the bar and be right back." She looked at Kara. "Okay?"

Kara shook her head. "I don't need another drink, so you can stay."

Charlotte took the hint and sat down.

Peyton glanced between the two of them and fixed his gaze again on Kara. "So, where is your fiancé?"

"He's on the road." She looked at Charlotte. "Where are they tonight?"

"Memphis." Charlotte looked at her cell phone. "They should call soon."

" 'They'?" Peyton asked.

"Charlotte is dating Jack's brother, Jimmy."

"Now isn't that nice for both of you? Two best friends. Two brothers. Yeah, I'm sure that's true love, or is it just convenient?"

"Stop." Charlotte's voice was hard, cold, not a voice she used often. "Can't you just be happy for her, Peyton?"

"Sure. I'll try. But let me ask you this before I leave." He took Kara's hand and lifted it to his lips, kissed the inside of her palm. "Don't you miss me? Miss us? What we had? I mean, do you really want a life where your husband is gone all the time, singing songs on the road and being screamed at by young girls all over the country? Do you really want *that* life?"

Kara pulled her hand away, wiped her palm on her jeans. "Yes, I do. That is exactly the life I want."

Peyton stood. "Guess that's your choice."

"Yes," Kara said. "It is."

He looked down at her. "I still love you, Kara. If and when you discover that this is not what you want or need, remember that I still love you." He walked away toward a group of men at the far side of the patio.

"Let's get out of here," Charlotte said, raising her hand for the waitress to bring the check.

Kara shook her head. "It's fine. He doesn't bother me."

"Dang, he bothers me." Charlotte shivered.

Kara smiled. "You know, it just makes me understand how much I love Jack. There is this peaceful feeling that comes with loving the right person, a calm I never had with Peyton. And it has nothing to do with what kind of life I do or don't want. It has everything to do with loving. Just that."

"Just that." Charlotte smiled now too. "Exactly. I mean, if I look at it all rationally, loving a man who is gone most of the time is not the best scenario."

"We can help a lot of things," Kara said. "But you can't tell a heart who to love or not love."

"No, you can't. But wouldn't life be easier if you could?"

"Maybe, but not nearly as much fun."

Their laughter blended into the evening, into the music, and into the night.

Hours before Charlotte and Jimmy's first true disagreement would occur, Charlotte and Kara were in the Seaboro Bridal Boutique. Charlotte was waiting in a room washed in white fabric couches, curtains, and wedding paraphernalia. Kara poked her head out from behind the dressing-room curtain. "Okay, if I come out, you have to be honest," she said.

"I always am," Charlotte said.

"Yes, fortunately or unfortunately, you are." Kara opened the curtain and walked out in her mother's wedding dress that the store had altered: a simple satin sheath that gathered under the breast in a crisscross pattern of crystals and pearls. The fabric hung to the floor, cream poured from a pitcher, flowing to the ground in ripples. "Is it too . . . old-fashioned?" Kara asked.

Charlotte shook her head. "No! It is so beautiful, Kara." Charlotte couldn't help but remember the last fitting when Kara had been engaged to Peyton and emerged wearing an elaborate dress that looked like a chandelier, and Kara had, for the first time in a decade, spoken Jack's name when she should have been speaking Peyton's.

Kara twirled around. "Mama was a little smaller than I am, so we had to add some fabric in the back." She turned to display a panel of fabric that had been sewn into the back of the dress to look like a corset, pearl buttons in a line like bridesmaids waiting to walk down an aisle.

"I'm not sure this dress could be any more beautiful," Charlotte said, curling her legs underneath her on the white slipcovered couch.

A commotion began in the outer part of the store, and laughter filtered into the fitting room. "I know that voice," Kara said. "Don't you dare let him back here." She ran back into the curtained area.

Jimmy, always first and always loudest, burst into the room. Jimmy in his blue jeans and black T-shirt, with his unshaven face and booming voice. "Okay," he said as he loped toward Charlotte, "there is my girl." He picked her up, twirling her around and squeezing her until she gently bit his ear.

"Put me down," she said, and then took his face in both her hands and kissed him the way you kiss a man you love and haven't seen in three days.

Kara poked her head out from behind the curtain. "What are you doing here? I thought we were meeting you at the restaurant."

"I couldn't wait one more minute to kiss these lips." He tossed Charlotte back as if they were on a dance floor.

Kara pointed at Jimmy. "Out of here. It's

bad luck for you to see me in the dress."

"That's only the groom who can't see the dress. Me? I'm just the brother." He took two large steps toward the dressing room and acted like he was about to fling the curtain aside, but didn't.

Charlotte wrapped her arms around him. "Go. We'll meet you guys in an hour, okay? I can't believe I'm saying this, but go." She made a shooing gesture with her hands.

He kissed her one more time, then left.

"It's safe to come out," Charlotte called out.

Kara emerged from the dressing room having changed into her jeans and white linen shirt. "Come on. Let's go."

"Wow, that was quick." Charlotte laughed and grabbed her purse from the couch. Together they ran out of the bridal shop to catch up with Jimmy and Jack before they climbed into their pickup truck.

"Wait on us," Kara hollered as Jack opened the driver's side door.

Jack smiled as he faced Kara. "Hey, baby," he said and held his fiancée. "You know how hard it was not to peek in there?"

"Thanks for waiting," she said, kissing him. "I'm starving. Let's go get something to eat. I want to tell you all about my photo shoot yesterday."

■ ■ ■ ■

The Oyster Shack didn't have an empty table, and the foursome ended up at the long bar, hollering up and down, voices overlapping as the friends tried to catch up on three days' worth of stories.

"Charlotte," Jack said, leaning forward. "You should have seen the crowd waiting for Jimmy's autograph outside the bar last Wednesday. Here we are in Nowhere, Virginia, and Jimmy closes with your song and the next thing we know, girls are everywhere."

Charlotte tried to smile, but the edges of her lips were shaking. "I'd line up for him any day."

Jimmy shook his head. "He's exaggerating."

"Oh, it's okay if he's not."

"Hey," he said. "Let's get out of here, take a walk. I want my girl to myself for a while."

With a wave over her shoulder to Kara, Charlotte left the restaurant with Jimmy, strolling down the long dock to the water's edge. They sat with their feet swinging over the incoming tide. Jimmy took her hand. "I'm so glad to be home. Tell me about the Carson job. Has she let up on you at all?"

They caught up on the facts and figures of a life lived apart and then Charlotte rested her head on his shoulder. "You know, I understand why all those girls line up for you. I just hate it."

"Seriously, Jack was totally exaggerating."

They were quiet for a time, one breathing in while the other breathed out, until Jimmy said, "Can I ask you something?"

"Mmmm . . . ," she said as an affirmative answer.

"Jack heard that Kara was with Peyton while we were gone. That the three of y'all were at a bar one night. Is that true? Say it's not."

"Who told you that?"

"Doesn't matter . . ."

"It's true," she said and lifted her head. "But not that way. He ran into us there and sat down to tell Kara she was making the wrong choice with her life. It was silly and stupid."

"What else did he say?"

"Do you really want to hear this? It's ridiculous."

He nodded.

Charlotte let out a long exhale. "He asked Kara if she really wanted this life — this life where her man was gone all the time. He said that the only reason we were all together was that it was convenient to have two best friends and two brothers dating. He implied she'd have a better life with him. After his tirade, he left. He wasn't with us for long."

"That's not what I heard."

Charlotte lifted her eyebrows. "What do you mean?"

"I mean, I don't think it was quick."

"Well, it seemed interminable to me, but it couldn't have been more than a few minutes, really."

"Oh," Jimmy said, but his voice held doubt the way a shot glass holds whiskey.

"You don't believe me?"

"I think sometimes we protect our friends."

"That's not what I'm doing, Jimmy. It really was stupid, and he embarrassed himself. So I'm supposed to believe that all those girls who flock around you are an exaggeration, but you won't believe me about this?"

"I didn't say I didn't believe you." He stood and left her looking up at him, wondering who he was and where the angry voice had come from. "I just meant that we should always tell the truth."

"I am," she said, hurt and confused, her pulse skipping beats. "Peyton was implying that Kara didn't really love Jack, that it was some old infatuation. That all of us were a convenience. He's completely deluded."

"How do you think you can tell the difference between love and infatuation? I mean, how would you define love? And are we just convenient?"

She stood to face him, hurt pulsing beneath her skin. "No. Of course not. What are you talking about? I don't know how to exactly define love, but whatever it is, this is it."

His eyes had gone as cold as his voice. "I don't think we need a Webster's definition, but maybe you're right. Maybe we don't know the difference. Is that what you've been trying to tell me, that you don't really know if this is for you? That you're not sure if this isn't just convenient, that this might *not* be the kind of life you want?"

"No, that's not what I said. You're misunderstanding. You're taking what Peyton said about Kara and making it about us."

He looked away, and in that moment the past reached up and behind him, ancient history weaving itself into the present, and made him act in a way that he would later regret. And like his father before him, Jimmy walked away from anything that would make him dig a little deeper, go a little further. "I think I just need some sleep. I'll try and catch up with you later."

"Don't leave, Jimmy." She reached for his hand, but he kept his fist closed and tight. "This is silly. You know I didn't mean that I don't know about *us* . . ."

"Let's not make this worse. Let's just leave it, okay?"

In silence they walked the long dock back toward the restaurant while Charlotte searched for the single moment where he could have possibly believed that she didn't love him, that she was confused about her feelings.

Jack and Kara met them on the front porch of the restaurant.

"Hey, bro," Jimmy said. "I've gotta catch some shut-eye. Drop me off at a hotel?"

Charlotte looked at him. "Hotel? Why are you staying at a hotel?"

Jimmy shrugged. "I'll call you later." He kissed her on the cheek with a kiss that was as distant as a star.

Jack glanced between Kara and Charlotte. "Okay, let's go. Kara, baby, I'll see you in about thirty minutes. I'll meet you at your cottage."

Kara nodded, but turned to her best friend as Jimmy walked off. "What happened?"

Tears filled Charlotte's eyes, the tide filling the marsh. "I don't know. One minute we're talking about Peyton showing up at the bar, and then we were on to the difference between love and infatuation, between love and convenience. Then all of a sudden he didn't believe me about anything. He thinks I'm not sure I love him or want this life with him."

Kara exhaled. "Yeah, Jack asked me about Peyton too." Kara sat on a bench and motioned for Charlotte to join her. "Listen, Jimmy and Jack, their history is complicated; I know you know that. But Jimmy has always felt responsible for Jack. If anything goes wrong with or for Jack, Jimmy thinks it's his fault. I know Jimmy doesn't talk much about it, but their dad still influences his mind and thoughts. Just give him a little bit to cool down. He'll see . . ."

"I hope so. I get how the past sneaks up and grabs us. I understand. But maybe he's picking up on how it takes me a few minutes to get into a comfortable rhythm with him again after he's been gone."

"I know," Kara said, knowing that sometimes there are no words to fix a situation, that sometimes a friend just wants to hear "I know."

71

Charlotte rearranged the swatches on Mrs. Carson's Christmas design board, attempting to focus on her mantel swags and wreaths, avoiding thoughts about Jimmy. But that's the thing with trying not to dwell on someone: the harder you try *not* to think about that person, the more you do.

She turned up her Norah Jones CD and poured a glass of wine. Maybe this wasn't the kind of life she wanted; maybe Peyton was correct. He'd been talking about Kara, but maybe the sentiment was true. Maybe waiting for a man who was constantly surrounded by other women, waiting for a man who wouldn't be there for her, wasn't the way she wanted to spend her days or her life. But the more she talked herself out of loving Jimmy, the more she *did* love him. She lifted her phone a thousand times, or maybe a million, and then set it down again. She wouldn't chase him down. She wouldn't talk him into being with her. She wouldn't beg.

She sat down on the couch, no longer able to focus on the demanding Carson job, and dug out her secret notebook, the one where she wrote the poems she would never show anyone. The poems about nature, love, friendship, family, and anything else that caused her to find the words she needed to unravel the way she felt. After playing with a poem she'd written about the incoming tide of a storm, her cell phone rang. She glanced down: *JS.* She answered.

"I'm an idiot," Jimmy said without pre-amble. "I just am. Will you even see or talk to me?"

"Of course I will." Her voice shook just enough to betray her feelings.

"Well, good, then let me in. I'm outside."

She dropped the cell phone without hang-ing up and opened the front door to his beautiful face. He hugged her and then fol-lowed her into the living room where she poured him a glass of wine. They sat facing each other across the dining room table; he pushed aside the Christmas photos and plans and reached for her hand.

"Charlotte, I am *so* sorry. I know you weren't lying. There is just this thing in me that rises up in defense of my brother and then I lose sight of everything else. I am so sorry I walked away. That is what I should never do, and something I promise I won't do again."

She nodded.

"But can I ask you? Do you think this is

love or do you think it's some kind of convenient infatuation?"

"I love you, Jimmy Sullivan," she said, her
voice sure and steady. "No, I don't know
how to define what that is. But then again, I
don't know how to define a lot of miraculous things. I do know that as I sat here trying to talk myself out of loving you, I only
loved you more."

Jimmy stood and walked around the table,
took her hand for her to stand, and then he
held her. "I love you too, Charlotte. I just
do."

5

Before he left he told me he loved me
and would come back for me. And I knew
he would.
— MAEVE MAHONEY TO KARA LARSON

By the end of the first week in December,
when the tides were higher than normal and
the holiday crowds were beginning to arrive
and clog the streets of Seaboro, the phone
call came in for Jimmy. *The Call*. It was Milton Bartholomew, ringing to ask if Jimmy
would consider joining Rusk and Hope
Corbin's Christmas tour. It seemed the
opening act had failed to show up for the
past two shows.

Jimmy, not quite used to getting good
news, was confused at first. "Huh?" he
asked into the phone.

"It's Milton. Can't you hear me?"

"I can hear you fine, but I'm on the tour
bus and it's loud. Now, what? You want us

75

to do that Holiday Jingle Jam thing again?"

"No, Jimmy. This is bigger. Much, much bigger. This is the world's most famous country duo. They set out on a Christmas concert tour every year, and they'd like you to open the concert with your perfect Christmas song."

"Um, Milton, man, I think you got me mixed up with someone else. I don't have a Christmas song."

"Yes, you do."

Jimmy searched his mind for some type of Christmas song. "Jingle Bells." "Silent Night." "Rockin' Around the Christmas Tree." He didn't want to seem the idiot, but he had no idea what Milton was talking about.

Milton coughed. " 'Unexpected.' Dude, I heard you sing it a few days ago. Are you dense?"

"Oh, that song. Yes."

"Yes, we're going to rename the song. Rusk wants to call it 'Christmas Love.' "

Jimmy's reaction was gut-level — he knew he was right and he was not going to bend. "No," Jimmy said. "It's called 'Unexpected.' "

Milton laughed. "I don't think you get it. This married duo — Rusk and Hope — are the most powerful couple in the business, and they're asking you to go on one of the most popular Christmas tours in the country with the Nashville Symphony. You're being asked to join to sing *this* song. They want to open the concert with this love song to Christmas."

"I get it. I think. But we don't change the name of the song to make it something else. It is what it is. A song about unexpected love."

Milton made a noise that sounded somewhere between a snort and a laugh. "I'll tell them you're in. Then we can negotiate the name."

"What exactly does 'in' mean?"

"Fame. Adoration. Money."

"Milton, that's not what I meant. Dates? Concerts? My band?"

"It's not your band. It's just you."

"Milton," Jimmy said. "The band" — he glanced around the dark bus — "and me. We're one and the same."

"Not for this, you aren't. What it means is this: fifteen concerts across the country. You travel in the band bus — not with the stars. Starts now and ends December twenty-third." Milton rattled off the names of some cities from Atlanta to Nashville to Sarasota. Then he told Jimmy the amount of money he would make for singing this one song and throwing in a few others they would choose.

Jimmy drew in a quick breath and glanced at his brother, who was sleeping in the bus seat next to him, his head back and his face squashed against the window. This money could buy them a new bus, new instruments, and a few other luxuries they'd been forgoing.

"I have to be in Ireland by the twenty-fourth," he told Milton.

"No problem. I'll email you the information, and I expect you in Nashville in two days. You hear me? Two days and by six p.m. for the first show."

"Okay," Jimmy said, but he spoke to an empty line. Milton had hung up because when Milton was done, he was done.

Jimmy spent an hour staring at the highway landscape streaming outside the window like a river in his private world. He was accustomed to this view — highway stripes, rest stop signs, small cars buzzing by, thin, tall pine trees lining the eight-lane like sentinels of the Southern highway life. The view around the bus was always changing. But no matter where he was or how far they traveled, the view *inside* the bus never changed: Jack. Isabelle. Luke. Harry. There hadn't been a lot in Jimmy's life that was familiar or stable, and when he'd found solid grounding — a home of sorts — in that bus with those people, it was enough.

How, he thought, could he possibly leave this band, his family, for a solo gig? But he'd said yes, hadn't he?

He needed to talk to Charlotte. There were moments when Jimmy was overcome with something miraculous in beauty or devastating in sadness, and both of these caused him to turn to Charlotte; she was the one he reached for first.

Jimmy took out his cell phone and, taking a quick, guilty look at his brother, moved to the back of the bus.

She answered immediately. "Hey, you," she said.

"Hey, baby," he whispered. "Can you hear me?"

"Yep," she said. "Is everyone else asleep?" She'd learned the bus routine — grab sleep when and if you can.

"I just got the strangest phone call," he said, staring out the window to see exit 14; they were now four hours from Seaboro. He knew almost every landmark that led from anywhere to Seaboro and how many miles stretched between that landmark and Charlotte.

"From who?" she asked.

"Remember that concert organizer? The one from the Jingle Jam?"

"Of course."

Jimmy recited his entire conversation with Milton. Silence filled the line, and he thought maybe he'd lost connection. "You there?"

"I am. I am. I don't know what to say — this is so amazing. Really amazing. Your song will be known everywhere."

"*Our* song."

"You know what I mean, Jimmy. You wrote it. You sing it. It's yours."

"But see, that's the thing. It's not really mine. It's all ours. Everything about it is ours. And I don't know if I want them to make it into something else."

"They can make it what they want," she said. "We'll know what it really is."

"Yes," he said. "Yes, we will."

"How far away now? Please say you're almost home."

Home.

Jimmy let the word echo through his inmost being. Home. He never, ever thought he'd again call Seaboro by that name.

"Four hours," he said. "I'll see you soon."

"I love you," she said.

"And I love you."

Jimmy hung up the phone and dropped

his head against the window, closing his eyes while the bus rolled toward Seaboro. Toward the love he now believed he'd never lose.

But here's the thing of it — we can all lose the most precious thing in our life if or when we forget its very value.

The temperate weather held out for Jack, Kara, Jimmy, and Charlotte to spread a picnic across the sand of the deserted barrier island and sit on blankets and towels. At a time like this on a beach, the sun warming them, the dolphins nosing around, the holidays seemed not to exist at all — only an idea.

Jimmy had all but fallen asleep on the blanket, that half sleep that allows one to listen but not participate. Charlotte's voice drifted over him. "Has Jack told you about the holiday tour?" she asked Kara.

Jimmy's sleep burst open to consciousness. He sat bolt upright. "Charlotte," he said. She sat next to him, her leg entwined with his like roots of a tree, their feet touching.

"What?" She turned away from Kara, who leaned back on her elbows.

"I haven't . . . yet . . ."

81

"Oh." She covered her mouth with her hand.

"You haven't what?" Jack stood and walked across the sand to the cooler.

"I need to talk to y'all about something." Jimmy changed the mood of the gathering that quickly.

"Nothing," Jack said with a laugh as he lifted the top of the cooler. "Nothing good ever starts with 'I need to talk to y'all.'"

"Well, it just happened yesterday, and I haven't yet figured out what to do or how to say it. But here goes." Jimmy recited the entire conversation with Milton.

The sounds of nature filled the air — a splash, a seagull cry, waves washing across the shattered shells like wind chimes.

Kara spoke first. "So you'll be done in time to get to Ireland for the wedding, right?"

Charlotte laughed. "I knew that would be the first thing you asked. And yes, he will."

Jack stood and walked to the shoreline, ran his foot across a thin strip of wet sand, and then turned and faced the group, his face unreadable. "Jimmy, bro, I am so proud of you. I want to say the right thing right now."

Jimmy stood and walked to his brother's side. "You okay with this? I won't go if —"

Jack held up his hand. "You've got to be kidding me. Not go? You must. This is so right and good."

"But the band. This will really mess up our holiday schedule. I mean, if I'm gone from now to the end of December, we can't do a single holiday party or concert. That's lost money. But I've thought a lot about it, and I'll make enough money to give the band double what they would've made with holiday gigs."

Jack reached into the cooler and pulled out the chilled bottle of wine that Kara had packed. He wasn't much of a wine drinker, but this moment deserved a toast. As much as the thought of not spending the holiday season with his brother almost broke Jack's heart, he was filled with proud pleasure.

"It's done then," Jack said. "There is no more discussing it. You'll do it."

Kara stood and walked to Jack's side. "This means you'll be home the entire holiday season. This means . . ." She bit her lip. "You'll be here while we get ready for the wedding. You'll be home." She exhaled the last word as if it were the most beautiful word she'd ever spoken, and maybe it was.

"Yep. Right here. Sometimes things work out, don't they?"

Kara cringed when she realized the good

thing for her meant loneliness for Charlotte. She looked to her best friend and smiled a sad smile.

Jimmy took Charlotte's hand. "You can come to almost every concert. I'll meet you in Ireland. It'll be okay. I promise."

"Of course I can't come to every concert," Charlotte said. "But I'll come to whatever ones I can. Let's just have fun today. The crazy begins tomorrow." She kissed his cheek. "I'm so proud of you. This is such a great opportunity. And yes, Ireland. We'll have that."

Jimmy turned to Jack. "We have tomorrow's concert together and then I'll have to go. We'll meet in Ireland."

Kara clapped her hands together. "Speaking of — can we talk about it for one minute? I promise I won't be a bridezilla and talk only about this wedding nonstop, but I just want to ask y'all a couple quick questions. I desperately need your opinion."

"You so don't need my help," Charlotte said. "This is your expertise. Planning. It's what you were born to do."

Kara bent over and picked up a small gray-and-white striped shell and threw it at Charlotte. "Thanks, pal."

"Hey." Charlotte ducked, then caught the shell in the air. "That was a compliment."

"Well, Jack and I really want to honor Maeve Mahoney at the wedding. If it weren't for her, we wouldn't all be here today."

Jimmy dug his feet farther into the sand. "I think getting married in her hometown and using a Claddagh ring for your wedding bands is more than enough. I mean —"

"Yeah." Kara sat down on the blanket and took a sip of wine from her plastic cup. "But those are more about me than they are about her. I want to go to Ireland. I want a Claddagh ring. I'm trying to think of something that is all about her, about her family and her story."

"Well," Charlotte said, "what meant the most to her?"

Kara stared across the sea, tried to remember some of Maeve's words and advice. "I think she cared most about how story opens our hearts. She cared about the power of story. She believed in angels. She believed in love returning. She thought we all lived the same stories over and over at different edges of the sea. She didn't believe we should hold tightly to life; she thought we should keep our hands open."

"Yes, all those things we honor by the way we live, I think," Charlotte said.

Kara's eyes returned to the group. "I got it: her words. Last year I wrote down all the things she'd said and taught me. I can find something in there to put into the vows."

"Perfectly perfect," Charlotte said. "See, you didn't need me at all."

"Ahya," Kara said, imitating Maeve Mahoney, "I just needed you to listen."

And yes, sometimes that is all we need.

Charlotte rubbed her thumb across the concave dip of the shell that Kara had thrown, then slipped it into her beach bag. She never wanted to forget this day, this feeling of the day being a love letter written just for the four of them.

6

For what cannot be cured, patience
is best.

— OLD IRISH PROVERB

The trees were barren and Jimmy spied a single leaf, shivering as if it were a living thing left alone in the frigid December wind. In Lexington, Kentucky, he sat on a bench in an empty park. Jack came and sat next to him and groaned. "The crowd last night was the absolute worst."

Jimmy shook his head. "You call that a crowd." He paused and shivered before pulling his scarf tighter. "So when does this stop being worth it? I mean, how long do we wait to break out before these gigs kill us?"

Jack shrugged. "I don't know, but I'm guessing we'll know by the end of your Christmas tour. If that doesn't change things, then we'll have to rethink all of this."

The iron bench felt like ice; Jimmy shoved his hands into his pockets. "Man, way to put the pressure on me." He smiled. "So, if my perfect Christmas song isn't so perfect, then we're all done for good?" He shoved his elbow into his brother's ribs.

"Yeah, yeah. Poor you having to go out on the fancy Christmas tour."

"You know, I could ask if you can come and be my irreplaceable manager."

"Thanks, but no thanks. Carrying your bags while fans swoon all over you when I could be with Kara? Hmm . . . Let me think about that one."

"I got it. You've finally chosen the girl over me."

"I can recall a time or two when you chose the party over me. And I won't have to think long or hard."

"Those days are over."

Jack hesitated and then said, "I talked to Mom yesterday."

"She okay?"

"She's great. But there's no way for her to make the wedding. She's just too frail to travel that far. I told her not to worry about it, but of course she's worried. I assured her we knew she'd be there in spirit."

A honk echoed across the empty park, and the brothers turned to see Isabelle standing on the bus steps waving at them to hurry. Jimmy waved back and looked at Jack. "All right, let's go."

Jack exhaled and stood, stared off into the winter day. "What city are we in?"

"Lexington."

"That's right. Lexington. Today you leave us and I go home."

They walked toward the bus and Jimmy shook his head. "Who would've ever thought we'd call Seaboro home again?"

Who indeed.

The sweet, sugary aroma of shortbread filled Kara's small white house, and Charlotte burst through the front door and called Kara's name. She clapped her hands together, as the cold had finally arrived. Charlotte wasn't prepared.

"In the kitchen," Kara called.

"I love this house," Charlotte said as she entered. And she did love Kara's home, with its whitewashed walls, crooked floors, single bedroom and bathroom, galley kitchen with room enough for only the essentials, and furniture that Kara had found in flea markets and antique marts, refusing family heirlooms when she was trying so hard to make her own way in the world.

Photographs of Christmas lights strung

across various porches, trees, and lanterns were spread across the round, ancient pine kitchen tabletop Kara had rescued from a rubbish pile and then placed on an iron base. Charlotte walked over to leaf through the photos. Kara appeared from the kitchen, dusting flour from her hands. "Hey, you."

"These," Charlotte said, pointing to the photos, "are amazing. What are you doing?"

Kara smiled. "I wanted to do a collection of Lowcountry Christmas lights. I took those pictures last year. Most are from around here, but some are from our trip to Savannah."

Charlotte picked up an image of a gas lantern with the lights winding their way up the iron pole. "I think I love this one the most. It reminds me of Narnia. What are you doing with them?"

Kara shrugged. "I think I'll add Irish ones after this trip and then . . . maybe next year I'll have a show?"

"Yes," Charlotte said. "Absolutely!" She nodded toward the kitchen. "Okay, I guess you started our gift tins without me?"

"You're only an hour late."

"Sorry. Jimmy finally called and I wanted to catch up. He's in Atlanta at the Fox. It's so exciting for him I can hardly be sad, but somehow I am."

"How was it saying good-bye?"

"Weird, honestly. I drove to Savannah and met some of the band. He's definitely not slumming it."

Kara flinched. "This is hard for you, I know. I'm sorry."

"At least I'm crazy busy with work. What with everyone wanting the perfect Christmas decorations, like Christmas is a competitive sport and the neighbor's envy is the prize." She sighed. "And there're only three weeks left. What's three weeks?"

"Nothing at all." Kara winked. "Want to help me decide which one to frame for Dad?" Kara slipped out another photo and accidentally knocked Charlotte's bag to the floor, the contents scattering across the hardwood: pens, notebooks, lipstick, hand sanitizer. But it was the notebook with the blue cover, faceup on the floor, that Kara picked up first. "What's this?"

Charlotte grabbed it and stuffed it back into the tote while they retrieved the remaining items from the floor. "My poetry notebook. You've seen them all our life. I forgot I had it with me."

"I saw it, my friend. You're writing more songs." Kara laughed and wiggled her finger at her. "You caught the bug from Jimmy. You've always been a beautiful writer."

"They aren't songs." A bite of anger flared up in Charlotte's chest. "Why would I want to write songs? This whole music thing — the tours, the nights away, the fans, the heartbreak. Why would I want to have anything to do with it myself? It takes Jimmy away from me. I'm beginning to hate the whole industry. Why would I want anything . . ." She paused. "No, they are not songs."

"Can I read some?" Kara held out her hand.

"They aren't very good, Kara. They are just a few lines to try and figure out how to deal with all this crazy." But she handed the notebook to Kara. "I just don't want to see you read them."

Kara placed her hand on top of the notebook and smiled. "Well then, I guess you'll have to leave, because I am reading them right now. I know how good you are; how could I resist?"

Charlotte rolled her eyes. "Don't you dare show them to anyone. Especially not Jimmy. He can't know how miserable I sometimes feel. It's not fair to him as he finds his way out there."

Kara held the notebook to her chest. "Just between us."

■ ■ ■ ■

Jimmy stood backstage and looked out at the empty Fox Theatre. He was awestruck by its lavish beauty, this theater built in the 1920s with a sky full of flickering stars and drifting clouds. A National Historic Landmark overflowing with artistic fantasy was a place a singer rarely allowed himself to imagine performing, almost too much to dream, too much to ask.

He'd only been in the theater once and that had been as a child in the audience. His mama had brought her sons to see *The Nutcracker.* The brothers had whined and wiggled through half the performance, but finally the happiness on their mama's face, the stars above, and the music had lulled both of them into silence.

Rusk and Hope Corbin were warming up on the stage, performing microphone checks and playfully arguing about whether she should or shouldn't take off her high heels halfway through the performance (which she had the night before). Watching this happily married couple filled Jimmy with hope, but also with a deep sadness. These two were so in love, and this made the tour a beautiful celebration of Christmas and love. But it made him acutely aware of Charlotte's absence.

Jimmy hadn't yet befriended anyone on the tour, and the loneliness felt like an emptiness, as if someone had come in and scooped out the middle part of his heart and told him he could have it back in three weeks. He was used to spending time with his own band — knowing every nuance, private joke, and hidden agenda — and here in this new environment he was just another guy. A guy singing one song and anything else they wanted to give him.

A backup singer — he thought her name was Ellie — came and stood beside him. "Hey," she said. "Isn't this the most gorgeous theater ever?"

Jimmy looked at her. She was young, maybe twenty-one at most. Her black hair was pulled into a headband, her face clean and waiting for the makeup artist. "It's beautiful. Something out of a childhood I never had," Jimmy said.

She laughed. "Okay, that's why you're the songwriter and I'm just the singer."

"What?"

"I said it was gorgeous and then you almost made it into a poem." She exhaled and shook her head. "I've always wanted to write a song, but after hearing your song during warm-up, I know there is no way I could ever write something like that."

"Of course you could. And I didn't write that one alone anyway."

She nodded but didn't seem to hear him fully. "Hey, listen. There're a bunch of us going out after the concert. The Vortex. Wanna join?"

"Sure," Jimmy said. "I'd love to."

"Great." She tossed her words over her shoulder as she made off to the makeup chair.

Jimmy took out his phone and texted Charlotte. I miss you. So very much I miss you. And I love you. xo

The concert went off without a hitch. Jimmy received his first standing ovation, and unscripted, the duo chatted onstage about the beauty of the song, of unexpected love and how Christmas was the echo of a long-awaited miracle. Jimmy watched the audience, especially the children, enthralled with the wonder of the Christmas lights, the orchestra, the sweetness of the songs, and the soft sound of jingle bells playing in the background.

At the end of the concert, tinsel fell from the ceiling across the stage, over the heads of the singers and orchestra. Jimmy didn't know how they did it, but the duo and the orchestra feigned surprise when of course it had been planned all along and had happened every concert before and would every concert after.

The curtain fell for the final time of the night, and Ellie stood next to Jimmy, pulling tinsel from her hair. Her black dress clung like a second skin, and her cat eyeliner was beginning to leak around her blue eyes. Her red-lipstick smile was wide. She didn't look so young anymore. "They love that," she said and plucked tinsel from Jimmy's shoulder.

He smiled. "Yeah, so do I."

She shook her head and her high ponytail swung. "You're a romantic for sure."

"Me?" He laughed. "I don't think anyone has ever called me that. Other names, yes. Romantic? Not so much."

"Well, you are. Your sappy song. Liking the tinsel."

He shrugged. "Guess things change before you even know it."

She exhaled and placed her hands on her hips. "I just think Christmas is so . . . forced. Everyone is working so hard to be happy. There are all these expectations for cheer and joy." She shrugged her shoulders, picked at her black-painted nails. "I'm glad to be on the road. How could anyone or anything be so happy and sweet for an entire month? I don't see how it can lead to anything but disappointment."

"I know," Jimmy said, swinging his guitar over his shoulder. "I've for the most part ignored Christmas. All this jingle belling is a little overwhelming."

"Exactly. It's like a magnifying glass — if you're happy, you're happier; if you're sad, you're sadder. And I think most are sad." She stared at the duo and nodded her head. "You think they could possibly be that happy all the time?"

"No way," Jimmy said and then thought of Charlotte and the way he felt every minute he was with her. "Wait," he said, "I take that back. Yes, maybe they can. I think that yes, it *is* possible."

She shook her head. "I don't."

He smiled at her, feeling a little sorry that she didn't even believe in the possibility. Ellie walked off and then called over her shoulder, "Meet us out back in twenty. Okay?"

"Will do." As he gathered his guitar and case, he realized that a year and a half ago he would have answered Ellie's question about being happy all the time in a different way. His cynical outlook would have joined hers, and he would have agreed. He plucked a few notes of his song and stared out into the empty auditorium. Even without a single person in it, the auditorium held a certain magic, a secret it wouldn't tell.

The bar was packed with people like a Jenga game, everyone jammed up against the wall and the tables. Flashing colored lights hung from the ceiling and walls. Plastic Christmas balls rattled from the fake tree to the sticky floor every time a patron banged up against it. The wrapped boxes beneath the white snow–sprayed tree were empty and squashed from the careless steps of those who crammed into the tiny space to hear the woman singer who looked as despondent as the Christmas decorations. Men and women battled for one another's attention, hollering over the singer, flirting, buying drinks, and faking cheer.

Jimmy saw this and knew it; falseness bore cynicism as its firstborn. He scribbled it quickly into his notebook and then shoved it into his back pocket. He placed his beer on the bar and stood to leave when Ellie grabbed his arm. "You're leaving?"

He didn't want to scream over the entertainer, knowing better than anyone in the room what it felt like to be ignored while singing and playing an instrument.

"Don't go," she said. "Everyone wants to get to know you. Come on. Just a little longer."

Knowing he must travel and live with these people, he sat back onto the stool and lifted his beer as an affirmative answer. The band and backup singers, the grips and crew began to motion from across the room — they'd secured a table. Ellie and Jimmy worked their way through the crowd, and Jimmy slid onto the bench, finding himself against the wall without escape.

Within an hour he was comfortable — this was the nomadic life he was accustomed to living, with the language of bands and singers and travel. He slipped with ease into the conversation and into the comradery.

Mickey, a crew member, sat across from Jimmy. "So, man," he said, lifting his drink to Jimmy, "you wrote that song for Christmas and that's what got you on this tour?"

"I did write it," Jimmy said. "With my girl."

Ellie hollered into the conversation, "He didn't write it for Christmas, though."

"Really?" Mickey laughed. "I wouldn't be telling anyone that little tidbit. They're all calling it *the* Christmas song. The perfect Christmas song."

Jimmy laughed. "They can call it what-ever they want as long as I get to sing it."

Of course, that's not what Jimmy meant, but it's what he said, and soon the power of what we say changes what we mean.

The secret tempo of music and being on the road soothed Jimmy until he felt part of the group. The bar closed at 2:00 a.m., and they walked out into the cold night and to-ward the Fox. The bus lights brightened the side street, and they all stopped for a mo-ment, waiting for the crosswalk sign to change to green.

"Home," one of the crew said, pointing to the bus.

"For now," another said.

They crossed the street, quiet, each one thinking of home and what that meant, where it was, and how they wouldn't be any-where near it for three more weeks.

Charlotte turned the pillow over to find a cold spot, checked her cell phone one more time; she hadn't missed a call or text. She glanced at the digital clock: 2:00 a.m. Jimmy usually called to say good night, but some-thing must have kept him tonight. She tried not to think too long or too hard about what that "thing" might have been.

She closed her eyes, but sleep still didn't

come. She finally stood and stared out her bedroom window. The sadness that arrived when she couldn't change a circumstance, when it just was what it was and there was nothing to be done about it, overcame Charlotte in the middle of the dark, moonless night.

The consolations she usually used to comfort herself — the reassurance that she'd see him in Ireland in a few weeks, that he loved her, that he missed her — weren't working. She flicked on a bedside lamp and picked up her blue notebook, began to write the words that kept her awake. "The Words of 2AM," she called the poem after an hour of writing and moving the ideas around. Then she set down her notebook, turned off the light, and rolled onto her pillow. "I miss you, Jimmy," she said. "Please come home."

7

The tongue ties knots the teeth
cannot loosen.
— OLD IRISH PROVERB

Morning arrived quickly for Jimmy, as he'd only been asleep for three hours when the bus pulled out of the parking lot and headed toward Nashville for that evening's concert. He rolled over on his cot and groaned; the curtain slid aside, and Milton stared at him. "Wake up, party boy. You're a star."

"Huh?" Jimmy sat up too quickly and banged his head on the upper bunk. He swung his feet out and, rubbing his head, asked, "What are you talking about?"

Milton waved an *Atlanta Journal and Constitution* Sunday paper in his face. "You. Front page of the Arts section. All about the new rising star traveling with the Nashville Symphony and the famous Corbins. But it's all about you."

Jimmy grabbed the paper from Milton. "Really?"

"Yep." Milton handed him a cup of coffee. "And you need to get your wits about you. I have over seven magazine and newspaper interviews lined up for you today — all on the phone, except for the live TV interview with *CMT Insider* at four this afternoon. So get your head together, get up, and let's get moving, superstar."

"This is crazy," Jimmy mumbled, taking a very long swallow of coffee. "It's one song."

"One song. That's all it ever takes, son."

Charlotte awoke to the ringing cell phone and stared at the screen. She hadn't slept most of the night, and morning had come with a blinding headache. It was Sunday morning, when she could sleep in. Who was calling?

She slipped her glasses on to see *JS* — his sweet initials. "Hey." Her voice cracked on the line.

"Hey, baby. Did I wake you?"

"Yes, but I'm glad you did. Where are you? How are you?"

"I'm somewhere on the highway, pulling out of downtown Atlanta and pointed toward Nashville."

"I wish I were there," she said.

"Oh, baby, so do I." He leaned over the phone so no one else on the bus would hear him, although he knew they'd hear parts of the conversation. For all the supposed glamour of band and concert tours, there was absolutely zero privacy. He didn't used to care, but now he did. He wanted to pour out his loneliness, his deep need to see her. He wanted to holler about the newspaper article and the CMT interview. The feelings were piling up inside him slowly but insistently.

They were both silent for a moment, in reverence for the love and the aloneness that could never be cured with a phone call.

"I have some good news," he said.

"Tell me," she said and closed her eyes. "I'll pretend you're lying right here whispering it to me."

"They wrote an article about me. Front page of the Arts section in Atlanta, and now I have all these interviews lined up. I'm gonna be on CMT this afternoon at four. Live. Watch it. They want me to sing the song. Our song."

"Oh, Jimmy," she said. "That's amazing. I'll be watching."

The *CMT Insider* hostess, Meagan, sat on a stool in front of the camera while a makeup artist applied powder to her face, added eyeliner. Jimmy glanced around the studio as if he were in a dream. He'd walked into the building wearing jeans and a black T-shirt with *The Unknown Souls* scripted across his chest. Within a minute, Milton's assistant, a raven-haired woman he'd seen with Milton a few times now, in tight jeans, boots, and a button-down white silk shirt, had given him a plain, black ribbed T-shirt with two buttons at the top and a gray cowboy hat. Jimmy slipped them both on and looked at her. "I would never wear this."

"Today you will." She smiled at him and pushed down on the hat. "You look great. Seriously great. You're gonna break some hearts this afternoon singing that song, looking like this. Just smile and do your thing. You were made for this," she said. "Made for it."

Jimmy shook his head. "You might be going a bit overboard."

"I don't think so," she said. "Smile now."

The producer, a tall man with a baseball cap, motioned for Jimmy to walk toward the couch where Meagan stood. He hooked a microphone on Jimmy's T-shirt while rattling off directions. "Okay, this is live. When Meagan starts to talk, look at her. Never look at the camera. You are talking to her and only her. When she casually asks you to sing the song, decline and then let her talk you into it. Say, 'Okay, sure.' And then you'll have exactly two minutes to sing."

Jimmy lifted his arm to allow the tech to slip the microphone cord into his shirt and behind his back. "The song is over three minutes long."

"Then shorten it, dude."

Meagan stepped forward. "Hello, Jimmy. I'm Meagan. Listen, no worries about the length of the song — just do your thing and the camera will cut off for commercial while you're singing. It'll give them a taste without the entire song, and sell tickets and downloads."

Jimmy held out his hand. "Nice to meet you. I'm a big fan of your show. It's a little surreal to have you interview me."

She smiled, motioned to the couch. "Sit and talk to me like we're sitting in my living room. Okay?"

"I don't believe I've ever sat in your living room." He grinned at her.

"Just like that. Be your charming, aw-shucks self and we'll be fine."

Jimmy nodded and sat, but the cowboy hat was pressing against his forehead, offering a dull headache.

"Six seconds," the tech hollered and

moved behind the camera. He counted down, and Meagan turned to Jimmy and smiled, mouthed, "Relax."

Jimmy smiled back at her. She turned to the camera. "Welcome back to *CMT Insider* new talent. This afternoon we're privileged to catch Jimmy Steele Sullivan on his whirlwind Christmas tour with the Corbins and the Nashville Symphony Orchestra. I know you might not have heard his name before, but after today, you won't be able to stop talking about him. I promise."

Meagan flashed her smile at the camera and then turned to Jimmy. How the heck did she know his middle name? "So, tell us, how has it been traveling on this Christmas tour?"

"A dream come true, honestly. A dream I didn't even know I had. The crowds have been enormous." He waved his hand in the air. "Now, I know those crowds aren't for me, but they're great anyway. I sing just one song, but for that one song, I can pretend they're all in their seats to hear me."

When Meagan laughed, he was relieved. He felt comfortable and didn't think about what he did next — tip his cowboy hat. He'd taken her advice to make himself at home a little too literally.

She laughed with him, leaning back and

smiling. "Well then, Steele Sullivan . . ."

"It's Jimmy." He laughed. "See? *No one* knows me, not even you."

"Oh, I know you. I like Steele better. And after we hear you sing, I have a feeling that some in the crowd will be there for you."

"Ah," he said, now flustered. "I'm out there with Grammy and CMA award winners. Rusk is in the Country Music Hall of Fame. I'm not kidding myself about who the crowd is there to see. I'm just there to open."

"We all want to know where you came from. Why haven't we yet heard of you?"

Jimmy smiled. "Guess y'all just didn't hear us in our neck of the woods out there in South Carolina."

"Is that where you're from?"

Jimmy shook his head. "Yes and no. We're from a little bit of all over. I grew up in Seaboro." He meant to continue, to talk about the band and Jack and Texas, about Charlotte and how she wrote the song with him, but Meagan had other plans and interrupted him.

"Now, I understand that this song has been called the perfect Christmas song."

He laughed and leaned back into the pillows of the couch, threw his arm over the backrest, and flashed the grin that had caught Charlotte by surprise the first time they reunited. "I think maybe one person called it that — and that's the manager — but it's nice to hear."

"No," she said. "I've heard this from several sources, and also from Rusk and Hope themselves. Can you tell us why you think this song has caught so many by surprise?"

"My brother, Jack Sullivan, and I have written hundreds of songs. You have to be willing to write lots and lots of bad songs to find one that rings true. I wrote this one with —"

"But this one!" she interrupted and placed her hands in the air as if she were scoring a touchdown. "This one is being called the perfect Christmas song."

Jimmy shrugged and glanced around. "Yes, well, it's about unexpected love. The kind that comes into your world and takes you by surprise. The kind that changes your life. The kind you didn't even know you were waiting for."

"Exactly like Christmas," she said. "When love entered the world in an unexpected way and changed lives."

Jimmy nodded and forced a grin.

"Well, can we hear a little bit of it?"

Jimmy forgot to resist, and reached down and grabbed his guitar, strummed a couple

109

chords. "Absolutely," he said, standing up and moving toward the standing microphone they had pointed out to him earlier. As he walked toward it, the camera shifted back to Meagan.

"Here, live from Nashville, singer-songwriter Steele Sullivan, singing his perfect Christmas song."

The camera swung toward Jimmy and he began to sing.

Charlotte, Kara, and Jack huddled around the big-screen TV in Thomas's Pub in Seaboro with the remaining Unknown Souls. When the station cut to a commercial about car insurance, the entire pub cheered and lifted their glasses to Jimmy Sullivan — a hometown boy. Anyone and everyone who'd ever heard of Jimmy Sullivan would now say they were his best friend in second grade or his girlfriend in fifth grade.

Isabelle was the only one not cheering, and Jack put his arm around her shoulder. "You okay?"

"He didn't mention the band or Charlotte or why he really wrote the song. He let them turn the song into something else. And what was that cowboy hat all about? And Steele? Seriously?"

"Isabelle," Jack said, "it's just a two-minute interview. Don't get all tangled up about it. He's not deserting Charlotte or us. And he'd never change his name. You know that."

"Do I?" She stood now, wrapped her coat around her body, and threw her scarf around her neck. "Listen, I gotta go. I'll see y'all tomorrow."

Jack turned to Charlotte. "Pay her no mind. She's always been sensitive about losing us. We're her only family."

The jukebox music blared now, and Kara leaned closer to Charlotte and Jack to be heard. "Yeah, she practically accosted me the first time I was on the tour bus. She asked me how I knew Jack and told me I had no right to be there."

Jack laughed. "I don't think that's exactly what she said."

"Well, whatever she said, that's what it sounded like."

Charlotte bit the inside of her cheek. She didn't want to admit it, but she agreed with Isabelle. Jimmy hadn't mentioned any of them. He hadn't said whom the song was for or what the song was really about. She didn't want to be the "sensitive one." She didn't want to pout or whine because her boyfriend was just on Country Music Television and didn't say her name. But something deep inside shifted, and she fought the rising tears.

"He looked cute, didn't he? Even in that silly cowboy hat, he looked adorable," Charlotte said instead.

"More than cute. Like a star." Kara leaned into Jack. "This is really great, Charlotte. Really, really great."

"Yes," Charlotte said, wishing she meant it.

Jimmy exited the studio and walked into the cold Nashville afternoon. The setting sun bit into his sight, the wind speaking words he didn't understand as it whipped around the corners of the tall buildings. He was alone, and the victory of that interview didn't taste as sweet as it would if he had someone to share it with.

Jimmy dug into his pocket, pulled out his paycheck. He walked down South Broadway, passing boot stores, bars, and restaurants. New bands and singers with sultry eyes and cowboy hats stared at him from bar posters taped crookedly to front windows. He stopped at the front door of Tootsies, where a band was setting up, and a bouncer placed his stool at the front door, preparing for the evening.

Jimmy nodded at him. "Who's singing to-night?"

"Not sure," the bouncer said, slipping on his baseball cap. "Want me to check?"

"That's okay. Just curious."

"They're all the same to me." The bouncer settled onto the stool and zipped up his coat. "Just another guy in another cowboy hat trying to get discovered. Singing about love and loss and broken trucks. The new ones all sing about being a country boy."

"Or about Christmas." Jimmy smiled, making fun of himself.

"Yeah, this time of year, that too. Christmas songs. Country Christmas songs about snow and being home, and like I said, it's all the same to me. Just give me a decent guitarist and I'm all good."

"I'm with you, man." Jimmy began to walk away and then turned back. "Hey, any idea about the closest jewelry store?"

"Two doors down on the right."

"Thanks," Jimmy said, knowing exactly what to do. The bouncer was right — it was all the same. What made this moment of fame any different from a moment of fame experienced by any other singer? What made *him* different? What made the song different? *Charlotte.*

It was time to tell her the reason — the

only reason he was now a changed man.

The bell clanged as he pushed the heavy door to enter the brightly lit store. A bleach-blond woman in all black with more jewelry on than one person should wear together came to the glass counter. Jimmy glanced around the store at the gold necklaces and huge carved belt buckles, at the dangling earrings and large rings made of gold and turquoise, stones bigger than a golf ball. The woman approached Jimmy. "May I help you?"

"Yes, I'm looking for an engagement ring."

She placed her hand over her chest. "Oh, this is my favorite. Finding engagement rings during the holiday season. You proposing on Christmas?" she asked.

Jimmy laughed. "Until about four seconds ago, I didn't even know I was proposing, so I haven't decided that part yet."

She pointed to a case at the far side of the store. "Follow me."

Jimmy walked behind her until he stood over a case of at least fifty diamond rings. "Oh, I guess I should have given this more thought. I have no idea what I'm doing. I don't know anything about this."

"That's why I'm here," she said, slipping a key from a chain and opening the case. She placed a black velvet tray full of rings on top of the counter. "Do you have a budget?"

"Yes," Jimmy said and quoted the exact amount of his first paycheck.

She smiled. "You sound firm."

"I am because I have to be," he said and smiled.

"Great. Well, here are the princess-cut solitaires. Or would you like oval or with baguettes?"

"Are you speaking English?" he asked with a grin.

"Let's start here — tell me what you see on her hand."

"A diamond."

"All right. Anything more specific?"

Jimmy stared at the tray, the diamonds becoming one mass of glittering confusion. He closed his eyes and tried to picture Charlotte, where he'd ask, what it would mean to her. His eyes flew open. "Okay, I'll be proposing in Ireland over Christmas. Does that help?"

She laughed. "Yes, yes, it does." She reached inside the case and pulled out a ring. "This is called a Claddagh ring."

Jimmy looked down at the platinum ring — the heart with the hands surrounding it, the crown above the heart, and a round, brilliant diamond set into the center of the heart. "Yes," he said, without knowing the word had formed itself and been spoken. He looked at the woman. "Yes, exactly yes."

8

We live our stories over and over in every
generation, at the edge of every sea.
— MAEVE MAHONEY TO KARA LARSON

Charlotte stood with Kara at the entrance
to the Verandah Nursing Home. This was
where Maeve had once lived, where Kara's
life had been changed by a story.

Charlotte placed her hand on Kara's arm
before she opened the door. "You think
Jimmy is okay?"

Kara released her hand from the door-
knob, her other hand holding boxes of
shortbread. Handmade garland was draped
over Charlotte's forearm. "Of course I do.
Why do you ask?"

Charlotte shrugged. "You know he's never
been alone on the road — he's always had
Jack and the band."

"You talk to him every day, right?"

Charlotte nodded.

"And he seems fine?"

She nodded again.

"Then what's wrong?"

Charlotte fiddled with the garland as pine needles fell to the ground. "I can't name it. I don't really know. Did you see that now they call him Steele? Not even Steele Sullivan. Just Steele. Like Madonna or Cher. One name. I hate it."

Kara brushed pine needles from Charlotte's hair. "You just miss him. It'll all be fine."

"Yeah." Charlotte forced a smile and opened the door to the nursing home. "You're right."

When they entered, they were overcome with the scent of disinfectant and baby powder. They walked back to the living room where the residents were watching *Miracle on 34th Street.* Mrs. Anderson looked up from her puzzle and smiled at Kara and Charlotte. "Well, well, look who the cat drug in," she said with a lisp.

Charlotte looked at Kara and whispered, "I've never understood that saying — what the cat drug in? What does that mean?"

"I think it means they didn't expect us."

The remaining residents turned. Some waved and others ignored them. Mr. Potter stood up in his walker and half walked, half rolled toward them. "Hello, ladies. I'm assuming you came to see me." He smoothed back the few hairs left on his head and winked.

"Well, I know I did. I'm just not sure about Kara here, what with her being engaged and all," Charlotte said.

Mr. Potter laughed and then spoke in that rough voice that told of his smoking years, of a scarred throat. "What gives us this pleasure today?" he asked.

"We brought homemade garland for the living room and a tin for each of you."

Mrs. Anderson looked up from her puzzle again. "What's in that tin? Did you ask permission from the front desk? I'm allergic to pine nuts, you know. And Dottie over there is a diabetic. And Frances, well, she can't eat anything that's been anywhere near shrimp."

Kara smiled. "It's shortbread. Just butter, sugar, and eggs."

Mrs. Anderson shook her head. "Now, how am I gonna watch my girlish figure if you're bringing me these treats?"

Kara placed the bag of tins on the table. "Well, you'll have to take that up with Maeve Mahoney. It's her recipe."

"Ohhh, you stole a family recipe?" Mrs. Anderson shook her finger at Kara.

"Borrowed," Kara said.

The nursing attendant entered the room and paused the movie. "Hi, ladies. You need any help?"

"I think we got it, but if you could just let me know if someone can't have short-bread . . ."

Soon the room was decorated with Charlotte's garland and ornaments, and Kara and Charlotte walked out of the nursing home feeling more joyful than before they'd walked through the doors.

The concert in Nashville was sold out. Jimmy's nerves almost got the best of him with the day he'd had, but he sang the song with the idea that Charlotte sat in the front row. They'd given him two more Christmas classics, and he belted them out with all he had. He felt silly — the new name, the cowboy hat, the tight jeans, the cheering crowds, the screaming girls.

Afterward he opted to stay in the bus while the band and crew went in search of a dark bar and tall drinks. Sometime in the middle of the night he heard them return, but his sleep was deep and silent.

Until the dream.

He walks out of a tour bus the size of a house; clouds are low and dark. He pushes and yet can't move forward. Finally he breaks free and attempts to walk toward the concert hall, yet obstacles are placed in his way — a gap in the sidewalk, a policeman not allowing him past, a wild fan grabbing at him. He pushes hard against it all, his head down, his muscles aching, his chest thumping to get to the concert hall, to the stage. Nothing else matters — not the crowd or the police or the gash in the earth big enough to swallow any man alive.

He sat bolt upright in bed and stared out the window at the Nashville parking lot. He felt he'd been sent a message, but not sure of what it was, he stretched back into his bed. He ignored that nagging sense of something important, something amiss, and he closed his eyes and returned to sleep.

There's a saying that time is relative. A very smart man said this and it's true — it's all relative to what you want and when you want it. Time seems to move slowly when you want something or someone, and it appears to fly at the speed of light when you're exactly where you want to be, doing exactly what you want to do, with exactly whom you want to do it with. There are also those times when it seems to stand still, to stop completely, as if time itself is holding its breath to see what will happen next.

Charlotte felt this way — that time was standing still. She looked at the calendar and counted the days until she'd see Jimmy, and yet the date never seemed to move closer. She kept track of his concerts and cities, but their conversations had dwindled from many times a day to every other day, with only a few texts in between.

Her client, Mrs. McClintock, stood at the top of her staircase and spoke down to Charlotte — literally and figuratively. "Young lady, you promised there would be freeze-dried pomegranates on this garland and that you would add a splash of red." The woman fingered the top of the garland wrapped around the staircase and slowly descended the stairs, one deliberate step at a time, emphasizing each word with the click of her high heels.

Charlotte released a long sigh, smiled through her gritted teeth. "I explained on the phone yesterday that the supplier is out of pomegranates so I used red berries instead. There is still a splash of red to accent the rest of your decorations."

Mrs. McClintock reached the bottom of the staircase but remained one step above Charlotte. "Yes, but this is the exact same garland as the one Edith Carson has in her foyer. And don't try to tell me it's not, because I was at her Christmas party last night. Now, what are we going to do about this? My party is tonight, and I cannot have the same exact decorations as Edith Carson. I just cannot. So, my dear, what are you going to do to rectify the situation?"

"Well," Charlotte said, "I can weave some dried oranges and some magnolia leaves into the garland and it will have a completely different look."

"Yes, *different* is one word. *Gaudy* might be another word. *Cheesy* might be another. Oranges? Are you toying with me? My decorations are red and white."

Charlotte kept her smile. She wasn't sure how, but years of practice helped. "No one has white and silver antique balls. I have a box of the most fabulous vintage silver and white Christmas ornaments in all sorts and sizes. I can't let you keep them, but no one, absolutely no one, will have anything like it. You'll be the *only* one. I was going to use them for the mayor's Christmas centerpiece, but if you want them, I'll let you use them. Your garland will be the talk of the town. Forget pomegranates."

Mrs. McClintock finally smiled, and Charlotte knew she'd hit the right button — one-upping the mayor's wife. "Perfect." Then

Mrs. McClintock scowled again, which was easy for her to do because once a face is used to being a certain way, it returns to that expression without any effort at all. "But," she said, "I need it up in the next two hours. You understand, don't you?"

"I do," Charlotte said. "I definitely do."

She walked out the front door of Mrs. McClintock's house and tried not to think about the other fifteen decorations she'd made and hung for the woman — none of which she'd mentioned. Charlotte ran her hand through her hair. She was slipping; she should've known better than to make two of the same type of garland for two women in the same social circle, but Charlotte had never been more preoccupied than she'd been the past two weeks.

She climbed into her car, turned the heat to high, and dialed Jimmy's number on her cell phone. She leaned back on the seat and waited, but his voice mail picked up. Again.

"Hey, baby. It's me." She paused. "I'm leaving a client's house. She was awful to me. Well . . . anyway, call me, I guess, when you can. I love you."

Jimmy looked down at Charlotte's number flashing on his cell, but he had a magazine interview in less than thirty seconds, and if he answered her, he'd miss the interview. He reasoned that he could call her when the interview was finished.

Milton came from the front of the bus and sat next to Jimmy. "How's it going?"

Jimmy stared distractedly at his phone. "Waiting on the *People* phone call. What could they possibly want to ask me?"

"This is for their Christmas issue. Just say what you've been saying all week."

Jimmy looked at Milton. "I'm starting to sound like someone else. All these interviews. I read them, but the articles aren't about me. I say these things, I know, but then they move the words around and make me sound like someone else. They're calling me Steele. This is getting absurd."

"You're complaining?"

"No," Jimmy said, running his finger along the mist that had formed on the inside of the window. "I'm just so tired. I just want to . . . sleep."

"Well, you'll be able to do that in the new year."

"The twenty-fourth," Jimmy said.

"Well, that's why I'm back here to talk to you."

The phone buzzed, and they both looked at it to see the 212 area code for New York City. *"People,"* Milton said. "Answer it. I'll be back when you're done. We're an hour from Raleigh."

Charlotte checked her cell and then made sure the ringer was set to On. Jimmy hadn't answered the phone in two days, and when he called her back it was usually the middle of the night. It wasn't that she didn't want him to have success; she just missed him. She slammed the gearshift into drive and headed in the wrong direction, which she didn't realize until she'd reached the stoplight and had that odd, disconnected feeling one has when that person has gone the wrong way, or has missed an exit, or is missing someone else so badly that the details of life become unfocused.

"Get over yourself," she said out loud.

But that's the thing about the Christmas season; it's hard to get over expectations. It's harder than any other time of year to get past "I want." It was not designed this way, though. It's supposed to be about gratitude and giving, but somehow the spirit gets confused and the "I want" takes over. But by the time Charlotte had reached Kara's house, she smiled when her best friend answered the door.

Like Mrs. McClintock's face that formed itself into its favorite look, Charlotte's moved back into its original delight.

Kara hugged Charlotte. "Hey, what's up?"

"I need to steal your vintage mercury ornaments for the night."

"Absolutely. But then you must help me finish sketching out the chapel decorations for the nun in Galway. She needs me to scan and email them to her by tomorrow."

"Scanning and emailing a nun in Galway. Something about that doesn't sound right."

"Right?" Kara laughed, which she'd been doing a lot of lately, what with her wedding now only two weeks away.

Charlotte turned her full attention to her friend and remembered the wedding she'd canceled. "The last time you were obsessed with every swatch of fabric, every bouquet, every smallest detail. You're so much more relaxed now."

Kara scrunched up her face. "Yeah, last time I think I was a bit more worried about the wedding than the marriage. Now I just want to get to Ireland, see where Maeve grew up, and say 'I do' in that sweet chapel."

"Oh, Kara, it's all so amazing." Charlotte sat in the whitewashed ladder-back chair. "Like a miracle. A real one."

"It feels like it." Kara sat next to Charlotte and held out a photo of the chapel's sanctuary. "Okay, so here's the picture. I told the nun I just want white roses on the end of each pew. The chapel is so pure I just don't think I want any other decorations."

Charlotte looked at the picture and ran her pinky across the edge. "What about some magnolia leaves on every other pew? You know, something Southern to hint at your roots. I can have them sent overnight. We can take them from the tree we used to hide in when we were kids."

"Yes," Kara said, jumping up. "Perfect. You're so good at this."

Together the two best friends huddled over the chapel photo and talked about flowers and travel and the Christmas they all waited for.

Milton returned to the bus seat just as Jimmy was dialing Charlotte's number. "How'd the interview go?"

"Same old, same old." Jimmy ran his hands across his weary face. "Can I have a few minutes alone?"

"Nope, sorry. We'll be in Raleigh in thirty minutes and I need to talk to you before sound check."

"What is it?" Fatigue pulled at Jimmy's eyes; his insides felt weighed down with concrete.

"Well, look at you. Someone lost their Christmas cheer?"

"I'm just tired, that's all. I don't think I can hear 'Jingle Bells' one more time."

"Well, you've got — let me count . . ." Milton ticked cities off on his fingers. "Six more times to hear it."

"That doesn't include sound check." Jimmy groaned.

"Well, I'm here to cheer you up. I have great news."

"Yes?"

"You have been invited to sing your song at *The Radio City Christmas Spectacular* on Christmas Eve."

"No can do." Jimmy held up his hand. "I'll be on a plane to Ireland by then."

"You aren't listening to me. You have been invited to sing at Rockefeller Center. Nationally broadcast. Christmas Eve. As of now, only the country music fans have heard your song. That night the entire world will hear you. Don't you understand? There are a thousand singers who would kill their mama for this chance."

"Can I think about it?" Jimmy asked.

"Yeah, sure." Milton paused and stared out the window. "For two seconds. That is how long you have to think about it because

I have to call the network and give the okay."

Jimmy looked at Milton's face. "You already confirmed, didn't you?"

"Yes."

"Then here's the deal. I'm on a flight to Ireland the minute my song is over. I mean the minute. First class. And you reimburse Mr. Larson for my ticket on the twenty-third. You got it?"

"Look at you, Steele, getting a handle on this star attitude." Milton smiled. "I think I like it."

Jimmy exhaled. "It's my brother's wedding."

Milton held up his hand. "If anyone could understand why you're doing this, it would be Jack, wouldn't it? It's for you, but it's also for your brother and for the band. *Your* band."

"Yeah," Jimmy said, exhaling. "I guess you're right."

Milton walked toward the front of the bus as Ellie came back. They passed each other and turned sideways to make room. She sidled up and sat next to Jimmy. "You look like you just lost a puppy. You okay?"

"I'm good. You?"

"Couldn't be better. I love this Raleigh stadium. You ever sang here?"

Jimmy laughed and shook his head. "I

sang in a bar in Raleigh. To six people."

Ellie smiled. "Well, you better get used to the bigger gigs."

"I think I am."

"You're getting used to all the attention?"

He shrugged.

"Seriously, you haven't been able to get out of the bus without girls lined up. They wait by the back door of the stadium after the concert. They try to follow us to the bars. Is it making you crazy?"

"It's a little embarrassing," he said.

"I bet you've slept ten minutes every night."

"Well, if y'all would quit dragging me out every night, it might be better." He laughed, but he knew he could stay back in the bus. And yet the two nights he'd stayed in, he'd felt the loneliness as a deep ache. He'd forgotten what he already knew — you can ignore your feelings, but that doesn't make them go away. They stay. And stay.

"Yeah, we're really draggin' you." She elbowed his ribs. "And we don't have to get up for the six a.m. interviews. Not that I'd mind."

"Good. Tomorrow morning you can be me." He smiled at his new friend. It was nice to have someone understand how crazy this all was. Jack, Kara, and Charlotte were back in Seaboro, enjoying one another, the wedding preparation, and the quiet. They could never understand.

She curled her legs underneath her bottom. "I don't think they'd believe me."

"So," Jimmy said, sticking his phone into his back pocket. "Tell me about your family. You haven't told me anything about who *you're* missing."

"That's boring." She tapped on the window. "Oh, look. It's starting to snow."

Together they gazed out the window and talked about music and bands until the bus pulled into the Raleigh stadium and the whole party started again. And that was what this had all become — a party. What began as an expression of love was fast becoming an expression of identity.

Ellie was correct — there were lines of girls waiting at every stop. The crowds backstage changed from children and families wanting to meet Rusk and Hope to girls in white tank tops and cowboy boots just dying to meet and touch Steele.

He stepped off the bus and signed autographs, shook hands, smiled for the cameras. He posed with Santa Claus in a sleigh onstage, as if the sleigh were real, as if Santa were real, as if the fame were real.

9

Here is where you must be careful: not all
things are as they appear to be.
— MAEVE MAHONEY TO KARA LARSON

The paperboy rode his bike through the
frigid streets of Seaboro, throwing the
plastic-wrapped newspaper over his shoulder with the same move he used for his fast-
ball on the baseball diamond — this was
how he practiced and made cash at the
same time. He hated this time of year not
only for the cold but also for having to
dodge the Christmas decorations people put
in their front yards, the strings of lights and
wires that caught his bicycle tire in the pre-
dawn. When he reached Charlotte's house,
he threw the paper, not knowing he was de-
livering news that should have come another
way, news that should have come from
Jimmy Sullivan himself.

Charlotte was already standing in the

kitchen holding a cup of coffee and staring into the beginning of a day when the thump of the newspaper hit her porch. She opened the front door and grabbed the bundle. Her mind on anything but the news, she unwrapped the paper and stuffed the rubber band in the junk drawer — just like every morning. The paper flopped open on the countertop, and she read the headline twice before she understood, before the words held any meaning. The announcement in the Seaboro morning paper was splashed in capital letters: SEABORO'S OWN JIMMY SULLIVAN TO SING AT RADIO CITY ON CHRISTMAS EVE. Her hand shook; coffee splattered across the counter.

She hadn't spoken to Jimmy in days and now she knew why: he was off in his own land. He was gone from her; she'd felt it, and now she *knew* it.

The article remained unread, the coffee soaking through the print as Charlotte walked into the living room. Really, why did she need to read it? The headline told her everything she wanted to know. He'd moved on with this new life, with the name Steele and the cowboy hat. He didn't care enough to tell her he was singing in New York City and wasn't coming to Ireland. Of course he wasn't. He couldn't be in New York City and Ireland at the same time. She plugged in her prelit, perfectly decorated but fake Christmas tree. She turned a key for the gas fireplace, threw in a match, and sat in the threadbare lounge chair, the one she'd been meaning to recover but hadn't yet because she loved the old faded chintz.

With her notebook in hand, she stared at the tree, at the gas fire licking the fake logs, and wished it were all real: the logs, the tree, Jimmy's love. But they weren't. And maybe none of it had been.

What is real? she wondered and began to write lines about the false fires we light and the spark of truth we might not ever see.

Jimmy awoke to his cell phone buzz. He groaned. He'd never been so tired. He glanced at the screen, but the leftover whiskey fogged his mind and his eyesight. He answered without knowing who it was.

"Hey, bro. What *is* going on?" It was his brother's familiar voice.

"Hey, I'm finally getting some shut-eye. Can I call you back?"

"Ah, have you seen the front page of the *Seaboro Times*?" Jack asked.

Jimmy's irritation prickled. "How would I have seen the front page of the *Seaboro Times* when I'm in Raleigh and I'm asleep?"

Jack's answer was silence, but it really wasn't silence at all. It was an accusatory hissing sound that Jimmy heard in his ear as disapproval. Jimmy exhaled into the phone. "I'm guessing you want me to ask you what it says."

"Oh, I'm thinking you already know." Jack's voice was low, rough as sandpaper, and Jimmy quickly understood Jack was angry. Now he was awake.

"Why don't we quit playing this stupid game and you tell me. If it was important enough to wake me —"

"Seems you're singing at Radio City on Christmas Eve. Singing your perfect Christmas song."

Jimmy rubbed at his forehead, wished he hadn't had that last shot of whiskey at the bar with Ellie. He groaned. "I was gonna call you this morning, Jack. I was."

"Okay."

"Milton said yes for me, and how could I possibly turn it down? This could change everything for us. For me. For you. For our band. It's nationally broadcast . . ." Jimmy heard Milton's words coming out of his own mouth.

"It's nationally broadcast, and oh, by the way, it's also my wedding."

Jimmy knew this, but sometimes the saying of something is worse than the knowing of it, and this was one of those times. "I'm sorry," Jimmy said. "Of all people, you understand, right? I mean, this is for both of us. For all of us. They say they'll fly me out the second I finish the song and I'll be there just in time."

"I don't think so." Jack's voice was quiet now, the anger gone. "Have you talked to Charlotte?"

"I'll call her right now." Jimmy sat up. Charlotte. He hadn't told her. His head spun and nausea rose.

"Good idea."

"Jack?"

"What?"

"Man, I'm sorry. Please try to understand. Please. Let me talk to Charlotte and I'll call you back in a while. I'll meet you in Ireland on Christmas Day night; I'll be there in time to celebrate."

"That's just great. Jimmy, always in time for the party."

Jack hung up without a good-bye, and Jimmy slumped into his bunk, popped two Advil, felt around for the Gatorade, and chugged it before dialing Charlotte's number. It rang what seemed endlessly before going to voice mail, and Jimmy didn't leave a message, because he had no idea what to say.

Charlotte heard her cell phone in the kitchen, but she didn't rise. Kara had shown up with warm donuts from the bakeshop and sat across from Charlotte holding her own mug of coffee. "Aren't you going to see if that's him?"

Charlotte shook her head. "No. I won't say anything nice right now, so I think I'll just let it ring."

The bright sunlit morning cut sharp and intrusive through the windows. "I'm so sorry. I don't know what else to say."

Charlotte twisted in her chair. "Do not be sorry. Not you. Listen, I knew what I was getting into when I fell in love with a singer-songwriter who traveled and lived in a bus. I knew, and I chose it anyway. It was sweet; now it's sad. But listen, this will not change your wedding or my excitement for it even one teensy-weensy bit." Charlotte reached for her second chocolate donut, took a huge bite, and smiled before wiping the icing from her lips. "This is absolutely and completely going to be the most beautiful Christmas we've ever had. I can't wait to get to Ireland. I can't wait to see Galway."

Kara swiped the icing off a crème donut

with her finger and smiled. "You are amazing."

Again a phone rang, but this time it was Kara's. She glanced at the screen. "Jimmy," she said.

Charlotte shook her head and Kara hit Ignore. Together they sat in silence, sipping their coffee.

10

A good friend is like a four-leaf clover.
Hard to find but lucky to have.
— IRISH PROVERB

A week had passed, the days fleeing as Charlotte kept herself in a flurry that excluded all thoughts of Jimmy . . . or Steele. She had helped Kara, wrapped gifts, decorated other people's homes, and packed for her best friend's wedding. Now the plane hovered in the sky with the miracle of flight that Charlotte did not want to spend too long thinking about. She settled back into her seat and flipped through the movie choices on the small screen set into the back of the seat in front of her. None sounded appealing. It was an all-night flight and she knew she should sleep — they'd land in Ireland at six in the morning and have a full day ahead — but her thoughts spun.

Kara and Jack sat two rows over, asleep.

Isabelle and Harry lounged five rows ahead. Kara's dad, Porter, and Charlotte's mom, Rosie, were in first class. Luke had stayed home with his family, and then there was the empty seat next to Charlotte — a visual reminder that Jimmy wasn't with her.

The morning the newspaper had arrived, Charlotte had decided to focus only on Kara's wedding and her best friend's joy. She would *not* think about or talk to Jimmy Sullivan, and she had mostly kept this vow until now, when the feelings of missing him crowded in on her as if a large, obese man were sitting in the seat next to her, shoving her into the window.

Jimmy had left numerous messages and texts. First he tried explaining, then apologizing; the last one was angry. Charlotte had never heard him use that tone of voice before, and she erased both the recording and the memory of the exact words. He'd spoken of her not understanding, of his need to help the band, of his own career.

She now reached into her purse and pulled out the shell that Kara had thrown to her the afternoon Jimmy had announced this tour. She'd believed then — believed in them, in love surviving a music tour, in a fairy tale. Her finger ran across the concave surface worn smooth by the sea, her sadness settling like smoke into the curve of the shell.

Outside, the sunset settled like ribbons across the line between cloud and earth. Her eyes closed and her thoughts quieted. She felt a presence and she imagined, for that moment between sleep and consciousness, between knowing and believing, that Jimmy was with her. She opened her eyes to see Kara.

"Did I wake you?" Kara asked.

"No, I think I just was sort of half-asleep. For a millisecond I thought you were Jimmy. That he was here."

"I'm sorry," Kara said. "I looked over at the empty seat and —"

"No. None of that from you. This is your wedding. Your time. I'm fine."

"You're always fine. I know that, but you're allowed to be sad *and* fine."

Charlotte ran her finger across the glass window. "Look at that sunset. It lasts longer up here, doesn't it?"

"Huh?" Kara leaned closer to the window.

"The sunset lasts longer above the clouds. I wonder why. At home if you turn around or get distracted, you can miss it. But not up here. The colors have been settling into the clouds for over an hour, lingering there like it's a party they don't want to leave."

"You," Kara said, "are adorable."

Charlotte turned to her friend. "You know, I thought it was so beautiful, a sweet attraction that would change everything."

"Are we still talking about the sunset?" Kara asked.

"No." She smiled sadly. "Isn't that what love is supposed to do? Change everything?"

"In a way it did. He wouldn't have written the song if he hadn't loved. He's just lost sight of it. That's all, Charlotte. He's lost sight. Jack is hurting too."

"No." Charlotte leaned her head back and closed her eyes. "You don't lose sight of love. Love isn't a sticky note you carry around and put on the most convenient place. It *is* or it *isn't*."

"You *can* lose sight. Look at Jack and me. I was blind to it until I wasn't."

Charlotte twisted in her seat to face Kara. "That's different."

"Why?"

"Because he didn't choose to leave." Charlotte shrugged. "Jimmy made his choice."

"As Maeve would have said, 'You must not demand proof to believe.' "

Charlotte turned to the window, the night now dominating the sky, obliterating east from west, up from down. "It's gone now."

They both gazed into the night; the sun

had settled to the other side of the earth where unseen forces were at work, forces Charlotte and Kara could not and did not see. As it should be. The calendar moved from December twenty-second to December twenty-third as they slept, and the plane slid across the sky to another land, another day, the minutes ticking forward in double time.

Jimmy glanced at his watch. He counted forward — it would be four in the morning for his brother and for Charlotte in that plane. The regret bounced against his fatigue, but he dismissed it as one would a bothersome child needing attention. He could not regret making a good choice for himself, and ultimately for his brother and their band. Charlotte had ignored him for a week, and he'd dug deeper defenses with each passing day. Why couldn't they all see the good in this?

Ellie sidled up next to him. "Okay, we're gonna go hit Memphis. Blue suede shoes. Elvis. You in?"

Jimmy smiled at Ellie. "No, tonight is for sleep."

She shrugged and turned to the crew. "Steele is too good for us now," she said, and her words held no mirth or laughter.

"Do not call me that." Jimmy's voice was hot with anger. "That's not it. You know that's not it. I just have to finally lie down."

"You can sleep when you're dead," a crew member called out, throwing a football toward Jimmy.

Jimmy dove for the ball, caught it, and laughed. "Good point. Let's go."

There was something about belonging that always captured Jimmy — belonging to a family or a group or a person. When someone grows up trying to find his place in a world where there is no place for him, a soul can sometimes be fooled into believing that it has found a place when really it's merely found a soft area to land that isn't his at all.

Jimmy grabbed his jacket and followed the group for a moment, trying to remember where he was. These cities were blurring together, all of them with auditoriums and fans and Christmas carols and Santa hats and lights. He wanted to call Charlotte. It was driving him mad that she wouldn't speak to him. He'd told Jack to please pass on the reasons he had to stay, to please tell Charlotte that of course he still loved her and this decision had nothing to do with how much he did or didn't care about her. But even Jack didn't sound convinced.

The group emerged into the dark, cold

night, and Jimmy glanced up at the sky where somewhere far away Charlotte slept in a plane flying toward Ireland. He slipped his hand into his jacket pocket and felt the box that held the ring he planned to give her on Christmas Day. He'd give it to her the minute he saw her; Christmas was just a day on the calendar, not one that was more or less special than any other day.

This was what he told himself.

Trays up, seats in an upright position, the plane began its descent into Shannon, Ireland. The earth drew closer, as if a camera lens were pulled in tighter and tighter, slowly revealing the greenest land Charlotte had ever seen. Stone walls spread like creeks and rivers through the land, dividing it into pieces of brilliant green so lush, Charlotte thought the color must have a different name, one larger and more expansive than simply green. If there was a land that could heal brokenness, it must and could be this piece of earth.

The runway rose up and the plane skidded to a halt. Passengers stretched and gathered their belongings. Charlotte glanced at her watch: 6:10 a.m. Midnight at home.

No, she thought. She would no longer compare there to here. Here it was a new day. The eve of Christmas Eve.

Kara and Jack waved from their seats and Charlotte waved back, smiled. Her best friend's wedding. This, she reminded herself, was what she should focus on.

Jimmy sat in the bar booth surrounded by the crew and glanced at his watch. The plane would be landing; they'd all be in Ireland now. He vaguely wondered if anyone had taken his seat, if Charlotte sat with a stranger or alone. Tomorrow everyone on the Christmas tour would go their separate ways and he alone would fly to New York City for the big event.

Jimmy leaned back and tilted his head. The flashing multicolored lights were giving him a headache. An itchy, threadbare wreath behind his head scratched his neck. He grabbed at the irritating wreath and ripped it from the wall, then tossed it onto the bench behind him.

Ellie looked over at the discarded plastic greenery and tilted her head in question, her hair falling in her face. "Have your parents ever seen you play or sing?"

"What?" Jimmy rubbed his neck.

She shrugged. "I'm just asking. Mine never have. They think it's a waste of time and that I'm squandering my life away."

Jimmy looked at this wounded young girl. "My mom has seen us a million times or more, poor thing. But I don't think my dad even knows I sing. Or play. Or that I'm alive."

"I'm sorry," she said.

Jimmy shook his head. "No big deal. It's been a long, long time since I've thought about it."

"Nothing like that is ever a long time ago." She touched his arm. "Don't you want him to —"

Jimmy held up his hand and shook hers loose. "Listen, I don't want anything that in any way has something to do with or about my dad. He's long gone and good riddance."

Ellie picked up the discarded wreath, hung it back on the hook behind Jimmy's head. "That's why I'm out here on the road during the holidays. So much easier than being home, wherever home is."

Jimmy lifted his glass of whiskey. "Exactly. Wherever home is."

Jimmy's irritation turned to anger as quickly as a storm turns into a hurricane, building strength, gathering cloud on cloud, rain on rain, fury on fury. Forget Charlotte and love and weddings. Forget his dad and concerts and family expectations. And seriously, forget Christmas. What a crock, believing that a single day or a single love or a single person could change anything.

When the bar closed, the band and crew walked through the streets of Memphis, bundled up and talking about going home in the morning. Milton turned to Jimmy. "You, my friend, have a six a.m. flight to New York."

"I know, I know." Jimmy exhaled. "I'm already packed."

They filed onto the bus and Jimmy walked to his bunk, lay down on the hard mattress, and, although he tried not to, thought of his dad. He pushed against the memories, but they returned like thunder in a storm that seemed far off but was actually in the backyard. Why, Jimmy wondered, was he thinking about the wretched man now?

If he didn't care about the old man, why was he wondering if he knew about the Unknown Souls or their mother or Jack or anything at all? Through the years he'd often imagined his dad reading about the band or their success, yet Jimmy didn't even know if his dad was alive, much less paying any attention to the whereabouts of his long-abandoned sons.

When he was younger, when they'd first moved to Texas, he'd imagined his dad reading an article and then calling, pro-claiming, "I'm so proud of y'all." Jimmy would dream of his dad in the audience, hiding, his eyes damp with pride at his boys' talent. But these dreams and imaginings had ceased long ago. Now, if Jimmy did think of his dad, he hoped his dad experienced regret and sadness. The need for his dad's approval was long gone . . . or so he thought.

But tonight, with Jack in Ireland, Jimmy felt the ancient need to have his dad know about his success and be proud. What was all of this for? This trip to New York City, this distance from the woman he loved, from his brother's wedding?

Approval.

He shook his head against the pillow. No way. It couldn't be. He was doing this for the band, for all of them. Not for his dad. That was ridiculous. He closed his eyes against the stupid thought and fell into the darkest sleep he'd ever had, ignoring the call of his soul's truth.

Their luggage came out in sporadic shifts and the laughing group of Kara and Jack, Charlotte, Porter and Rosie, Isabelle and Harry counted the bags until they were sure they had everything. Squinting into the morning sun, they emerged from the airport and into a sun that seemed filtered and washed in green light.

"Ireland," Charlotte said.

Kara lifted her face to the biting wind. "Wow."

"I thought it was supposed to be all gloomy and dark here in the winter." Charlotte extracted her sunglasses from her bag.

The group raised their eyes to the clear sky. "It is freezing, though." Jack pulled his scarf tighter. "Okay, let's go find the rental car place. I booked a van for all of us."

After deciphering the signs and tumbling aboard a bus, they emerged at the rental car booth and then followed Jack to the van. When they saw the vehicle, the laughter was simultaneous and free. The van was squat, square, and small enough to fit in the back of Porter's pickup truck at home in South Carolina.

"This," Jack said, "is what they call a van? We're going to need another car."

Isabelle sat on her suitcase. "No way I'm driving. I can barely drive down the right side of the road, much less the left side. Plus, I heard these are the skinniest, windiest roads in the world. I'll kill someone."

Jack laughed. "I wouldn't let you drive. But someone is going to have to pony up. I can't drive two cars. This is the largest they have, and there is no way we're going to fit unless we leave the luggage and strap Porter to the roof."

Mr. Larson coughed. "I know it should be me, but I've never driven on the wrong side of the road."

"Dad?" Kara poked at him. "Except that time in Charleston when you went down a one-way street and almost killed all of us."

"Exactly," Mr. Larson said. "But I can try."

"It'll be an adventure." Charlotte clapped her hands together.

"That's what I'm afraid of." Mr. Larson dropped his backpack. "I'll be right back."

The curving streets wound through the stone-dotted landscape an hour and a half north of the Shannon airport and into Galway. Charlotte rode with Kara and Jack, her feet crammed underneath the seat to catch the meager heat coming from the floor vents. Together they tried to pronounce every sign they passed — Cappafeean, Ardrahan, and Kilcolgan — laughing at their efforts. Green lumps of land pushed their way through dirt and stone, resilient against a ragged landscape. The stones and rocks echoed a permanence born in another time, a time so ancient that the person who had set these stones into walls could not have imagined cars or the people in them. A time long gone. *Yes,* she thought, *it all passes — love, joy, and sadness. It is there and then it's gone, leaving behind only the echo.*

She wiped at her eyes, forced her thoughts to happier things. "Pictures won't catch this," she said from the back seat.

Jack slammed on the brakes. "Hold on," he hollered, suitcases sliding forward, the car skidding sideways as they came to a full stop. In the street two stray sheep stood in the middle of the road, staring at the car accusingly, as if the car had driven onto their field.

Charlotte burst out laughing. "They just stand in the middle of the road and expect to not get run over?"

"Yeah." Kara rolled down her window. "They're looking at us like we're the crazy ones." She waved her hand out the window. "Shoo," she hollered.

"Shoo?" Jack's words were wrapped in laughter. "Did you just yell 'shoo' at the sheep?"

"I did," Kara said. "You have a better plan?"

Jack pressed his hand on the steering wheel and a tinny, small noise erupted from the car, a honk that really wasn't a honk at all but an irritating noise. Charlotte and Kara looked at each other in the way that friends do and burst into laughter.

Jack stared at them and shook his head. "You think this is funny?"

"That is the absolute most pitiful honk I have ever heard. My shoo scared them more than that."

A squeal of tires came from behind as Mr. Larson slammed on his brakes and just missed hitting them. Everyone piled out of the cars. Kara walked toward the side of the road, waving at the sheep to follow her, which of course they didn't. "Oh . . . ," she said and turned to the group. "Come here." Her voice held a reverential awe.

Then they all saw it: Galway Bay. The place Maeve had always described, where her ashes had been spread and her spirit hovered.

"Look," Kara cried out, grabbing Jack's elbow.

Jack glanced to the left and his breath caught. Only a dead man would not lose his very breath at this sight. Together the group gathered at the cliff's edge, high above the rocks, waves, and sway of the bay.

The late-morning sunlight scattered across the waves in a shifting pattern of the earth's motion, an intricate ballet. Boats bobbed like toys in the powerful force, waves slammed and scattered against the cliffs, then gently, impossibly flowed back into the sea that had just hurled them into the rocks. Like love, Charlotte thought. Going back for more, only to be tossed onto the rocks again.

Kara took Jack's hand. "How is it possible that it is more beautiful than I imagined?"

He didn't answer because he didn't have an answer. He kissed Kara right there over-looking the cliffs. "I love you, Kara. I do so love you. If it took a legend from this place to bring you to me, I will love it also."

Kara rested her face on Jack's sweater and exhaled into the wool of his scarf. "I love you too."

He leaned down to speak softly, so as not to hurt Charlotte's feelings. "I wish Jimmy were here."

She lifted her face and stood on her toes to whisper, "I know. You didn't have to say it. I know." She kissed the edge of his ear.

Porter looked at his daughter. "Weird how the sheep stopped us right here, right at the first view of the bay."

Kara laughed. "Yeah, you'd think Maeve Mahoney had something to do with it, wouldn't you?"

Isabelle hollered into the wind. "Now, I

have to admit this is one of the most beautiful sights I've ever seen, company included, but I'm freezing my arse off. Can we see this view from inside a hotel with a warm drink?"

"Arse?" Harry asked. "Who says arse?"

Isabelle shrugged, pulled her scarf around her head and face. "When in Ireland, speak as the Irish."

"Okay," Harry said as they all ran back to the car. "The first Irish guy I meet, I'm asking him if they say arse. Twenty dollars they do not."

Holy laughter rolled across the bay as they all climbed into their cars and finally drove up Dublin Street and into the Claddagh Village. The village of the myth, the village of Maeve Mahoney, the village where Jack would finally wed his childhood sweetheart, Kara Larson.

The bedraggled group stood in front of the Dominican church, staring up at the stone structure. Kara squeezed Charlotte's hand. "This is it."

Mr. Larson spoke first. "So this is the church Maeve told you about?"

The frigid wind blew in off the bay behind the crowd, but sometimes the sight in front of your eyes can take your mind off other sensations. This very church had been there for over five hundred years. It was called St. Mary on the Hill, a sacred site of the Claddagh Dominicans. Built of Galway granite, it was the presence of God in the village, more, oh how much more, than so many tons of granite and stone. The building stood broad and proud, light pouring out from her tall windows and side doors. Her reflection shone off the water as if there were a church beneath the church, a holy place on which the holy place rested. At the top of the church a statue of Mary was tucked into a marble enclave, a home of sorts. Mary stared out over the bay and at everyone who entered the front door. But there was another Mary, one the village called "Our Lady," and she was inside.

Kara turned to her friends, to her dad. "This is it. And it's more beautiful, like everything else here, than I imagined. This is where they do the blessing of the bay Maeve told me about. Every year, on a Sunday in mid-August, the entire town comes to the Claddagh pier here for the blessing of the bay and its fishermen. The priest reads and sprinkles holy water. I can almost see it from the story Maeve told me. The brown sails, the priest, the hymns."

"Can you tell us the story inside?" Isabelle asked with laughter hidden in her words. "I'm freezing."

"We're meeting a nun tomorrow afternoon for the rehearsal, but if y'all want to go in now . . ."

Isabella stood at the double wooden doors, opened them, and swept her hand toward the inside. "It's warm in here."

The church doors opened into a narthex and then an aisle leading to an ornate arched stained-glass window, where St. Thomas Aquinas and St. Dominic looked out with an adoring gaze. Arched columns and intricate mosaics lined the sides of the church, running alongside the pews like children keeping tight to their parents. But it was the wooden baroque statue that caused the group to stop, as though Mary herself had reached out and grabbed them.

"This statue," Kara said as she pointed at the wooden statue of Mary holding her son, "was in Maeve's story. I can't believe I'm finally looking at it. In a way I'm stunned it's real. That it's here. It's like waking up and finding part of your dream standing in front of you."

"What part of her story?" Charlotte stepped forward, fascinated with this statue in a way she didn't understand.

"Well, she is called Our Lady of Galway.

Maeve told me the Spanish priests brought her back from exile, along with the first rosaries. She was cleaned in Dublin and brought here with a huge parade and celebration. Maeve was in the procession that brought the statue to the church; she was with the boy she loved — Richard, the man her story was all about. Maeve said she prayed to *this* Mary to bring him back safely. I feel a bit like Alice in Wonderland wondering what's real and what's not."

"Hey," Jack said. "I'm real. Back to me, okay?" His voice held that sweet laughter Kara had loved since memory of him had begun.

She looked at him. "Sometimes I'm not even sure you're real."

Mr. Larson coughed. "Well, if none of this is real, then I don't have to pay for it, right?"

Kara smiled and pointed to the glittering mosaic behind the statue. "That is the blessing of the bay. She watches over that also."

The group slowly walked away and toward the sacristy, but Charlotte stood with the Our Lady of Galway statue. Mary cradled baby Jesus in the crook of her left arm, while three angels' faces set into the wooden base peeked out from under her garment. Her gown billowed as though a strong wind was blowing in from the bay. Her gaze was slightly askance toward her son, but also toward the world and Charlotte. Baby Jesus's face was placid and somehow simultaneously ancient and innocent; he held out his right hand, waving or blessing or maybe even stopping someone from coming near. A long mother-of-pearl rosary hung from Mary's fingers, which were curled in a delicate gesture. At the end of the rosary chain, an ornate cross dropped a tear in front of the angels' faces.

Charlotte stepped back. "So, what do you think about what we've all done with your son's birthday? I bet you have a thing or two to say about it, don't you?"

Mary didn't answer but gazed out, holding tight to her son. Charlotte imagined her answer. *"My love is for him and for the world he will serve."*

Charlotte glanced behind her to make sure no one else heard her and then she whispered to Mary, "I know you're busy being a mom and all, and that this is a crazy time of year for you, but if you have any influence over things, could you bring Jimmy to his senses? Let him know that this birthday, this birthday of your son's, is about so much more than fame and parties. Please let him know it's about love."

Charlotte reached into her purse and set

the small gray-white shell at the base of the statue right next to the angels' placid faces.

11

You must not demand proof to believe.
— Maeve Mahoney to Kara Larson

The Irish pub was warm, the lights dim, and the group of travelers struggled to keep their eyes open. Their rooms weren't prepared yet, and they'd all agreed to stay awake until at least dark, when they could crash and start fresh in the morning, but they were fading quickly.

"Okay," Kara said. "Let's finish talking about plans. That way we'll all stay awake."

"Yeah, that always makes me stay wide awake," Jack said. "Logistics."

She pushed at him and he fell off the bench of the pub booth and landed on the floor, sprawled and laughing. "I think I just landed on my arse."

The blond waitress came toward them, ponytail swinging, and looked down at Jack on the floor. "Okay, should we cut him off this early?" Her Irish accent added a note to each syllable.

Jack jumped up and shook his head at the waitress. "Don't pay any attention to them. They've been flying all night and they thought pushing me to the floor on my arse was a funny joke."

"Arse?" she asked.

Harry leaned across the scarred bar table. "You can settle a bet here once and for all. Do the Irish say arse?"

"Well, that depends on who you ask, I'd say." The waitress smiled at them, glancing from one to the next. "Where are you from?"

"Seaboro, South Carolina," Kara answered as she scooted over to allow Jack back onto the bench, kissing his cheek and mouthing, "Sorry."

He pinched the end of her nose and then glanced back at the waitress. "We're here for a wedding."

"Ah, so I've heard," she said. "You must be the couple from the States getting married on Christmas Day in the church here."

"That we are," Kara said.

"How grand. A thousand welcomes. From what I hear, old Maeve Mahoney had something to do with this."

"That she did," Jack said, attempting to

imitate her Irish lilt and sounding a bit more like he was trying to imitate a Jamaican accent.

"Oh," Harry hollered across the table, "I wouldn't be trying that accent again, my man."

The waitress shook her head. "Okay, I'm Moira. Tell me what you need."

"Sleep," Charlotte called out.

"Well, you won't be getting any of that in here, what with the Shenanigans going on soon."

"The what?"

"That's the name of the band coming to play any minute. If you can sleep through them, you can sleep through anything."

While they waited for their food and drinks, Kara rattled off the last-minute plans. "So, we'll have a quick rehearsal before the Christmas Eve mass, and then we'll have dinner at the hotel restaurant. Then the bride will get her beauty sleep, and we'll meet at the church by ten Christmas morning." She glanced at Charlotte. "Do you think those magnolia leaves showed up?"

"What leaves?" Jack asked.

Kara smiled at him. "It's a surprise. I'll explain later."

After a round of drinks and fish and chips, the band did indeed come in, set up their fiddles and guitars, and begin to play Irish music that filled the room and the souls of everyone at the table.

"Wow," Kara hollered across to Charlotte. "Jimmy would love these guys."

Charlotte gave a sad smile. "Yeah, I bet he would."

Kara slapped her hand over her mouth. "I'm such an idiot. That's what no sleep does to me. I'm sorry."

Charlotte shook her head. "No, you're right. He'd love them."

Jack reached across the table and squeezed her hand but didn't say a word. The dancing had started up full force and voices were buried beneath the stomps, laughter, and fiddle. A man from the crowd reached down and grabbed Charlotte, pulling her into the pressing and dancing throng.

Charlotte was dizzy with the Guinness, the sleepless plane ride, and the loud music, and she protested, but to no avail. The man with the dark beard, blue eyes, and craggy face of a fisherman took her onto the dance floor and twirled her in circles, laughing. When they began a song Jack knew, he sang the words and danced around Kara, Charlotte, and the unknown man.

Isabelle watched this scene from the bench and tears filled her eyes. Jimmy should be here for his brother, for this magical and mystical moment when they danced at the edge of a bay in another land. She grabbed Jack's cell phone, took a quick picture, and texted it to Jimmy. Then she erased the photo and snuck Jack's phone back into his coat pocket.

Harry leaned over. "What did you just do?"

"Showed that ole Jimmy Sullivan that he's a fool. A big, grand fool."

"Isabelle . . ." His voice trailed off like a father reprimanding a child.

She held up her hand. "You be minding your own business now."

He laughed. "You, my dear, can't do an Irish accent any better than Jack. Now, get up and dance with me."

And they did, and then so did Porter and Rosie. They all danced to the lyrics and melody of an ancient time, an old Claddagh song sung in Gaelic, words they only understood in their hearts.

The streets of New York City were packed, making Jimmy feel invisible. The noon sun beat down and yet it held no warmth, the air frigid and still.

He glanced at his cell phone, and although he knew it was futile, he hoped Charlotte had called from Ireland. If she hadn't returned his texts when she was in South Carolina, why would she call from another country across the sea?

Jimmy scrolled and saw a text from Jack, but he didn't open it. As the crowd pushed him toward Rockefeller Center, he allowed himself to be carried along like flotsam on the tide and then stood in front of the famous Christmas tree. He knew the tree was huge, but photos didn't do it justice; its size was beyond his expectations. Thousands of lights flickered in the thick and widespread branches. Bulbs the size of his head were bobbing in the wind. A fence surrounded the tree and Jimmy stood staring, glancing up and down, unable to see the entire tree at once. A commotion of voices and laughter bubbled up to the right and Jimmy turned. A bearded man held his hands up in the air and hollered, "She said yes!"

Laughter and clapping resonated, and even Jimmy found himself smiling. This total stranger had just proposed to his love, and yet the anonymous crowd joined in the joy as though they all needed a reason to celebrate. His chest ached with loneliness, and he stepped back from the fence, turned away from the celebration. He'd just go to bed, sleep until his performance tomorrow, and then go straight to those he loved.

He could make it another two days. Yes, he could. He gritted his teeth. He would make up for his absence. He would find a way.

The hotel was warm and inviting, the bundled-up doorman opening the glass doors and welcoming Jimmy into the foyer where a fireplace and a Christmas tree cuddled up next to a menorah.

He checked into his room, then threw his backpack onto the floor. After ordering pizza and a shot of whiskey from room service, he stared out the window and watched the crowd below, thought about how everyone had their own pain, their own demons, their own sleepless nights and haunted choices. He thought of how he'd probably lost Charlotte with his own choices, yet still his emotions swung from anger to loss to hope.

He sat on the bed and took the notepad off the faux mahogany desk and wrote the first lyrics that came to him.

I can't tell my heart what to do.
I can't demand it stop loving you.

He wrote until his eyes wouldn't stay open, then he checked his cell phone one more time — hoping, yes, still hoping — and closed his eyes.

Charlotte and Kara stood at the threshold of the door to their Claddagh hotel room and their laughter started at the exact same moment. "Are you kidding me?" Kara asked. "That's a bed?"

"They look like those bunks we stayed in when we went to that awful camp in North Carolina in high school." Charlotte entered the room, threw her purse onto a chair. "But look at that view."

Kara walked to the window and together they stared out to the bay, to the long-necked swans dancing on the water as if they were at a formal affair in their finery. "Wow," Kara said. "I'm so tired I bet I could sleep on the floor at this point anyway."

"What a great day and night," Charlotte said. "I love when there's a wide-open day like that and you don't know what could possibly happen and then only the best things in the world happen and not one of them was planned."

Kara shook her head. "I love you for a million reasons, but here right now is one of them. I know you're sad. I know you miss Jimmy, but here you are looking at our day through the lens of joy."

"I am sad, but this day was like a little miracle in the middle of ordinariness." Charlotte ran her finger down the windowpane. "You know?"

"Yes, I do," Kara answered.

They each fell back onto a bed and Kara mumbled, "I don't think I can even get up to brush my teeth." But Charlotte didn't answer because she was already asleep, her breathing even and quiet on top of the down comforter where she lay fully dressed.

Jimmy Sullivan's hotel room phone rang its jangly, broken sound. Confused and disoriented about his whereabouts and the time, city, or day, Jimmy fumbled for the earpiece until his hand landed on the cold case and he lifted it to his ear. "What?"

"Mr. Sullivan?"

"Yes," Jimmy answered, clearing his throat in case this was the press.

"Your father is down here, and he says he needs to see you. May I give him your room number?"

"I think you've got the wrong room. I don't have a dad."

"I'm sorry to bother you, Mr. Sullivan." The operator hung up, and Jimmy rolled back into the pillow with a groan. He'd been sound asleep, something he'd longed to do for a month now. The phone rang again and he groaned once more.

"Hello," he said, glancing now at the clock: 11:00 a.m. He quickly estimated it was five in the evening in Ireland — Christmas Eve.

"Sir, this is the front desk again, and I'm sorry to bother you, but this man has shown his ID and is insistent that he is related to you and needs to see you."

"Can you put him on the phone?"

There were fumbling noises and then Jimmy heard the gruff, gravelly voice he would have known after a million years or more. "Jimmy, son, it's me." There was a long pause as this man's voice traveled from childhood to adulthood. Then he spoke again. "Your dad. It's me."

Jimmy's instinct was to hang up, but his hand shook and he sat up in bed. "What?"

"Listen, I know this is crazy. But I'm in the lobby. Can you come down and see me?"

"No," Jimmy said and stared around the room. Where was he? New York. Yes, New York.

"Son, I've been looking for you for ages. Just give me five minutes."

Jimmy's heart raced. He rubbed his fore-

171

head, stood, and opened the curtains. Sunlight flashed off high-rise windows, lit window answering lit window in some secret language. "Five minutes. That's it."

"Got it. Thanks, son," the voice from the past said.

Son.

When was the last time he had been called son by his dad? Jimmy rubbed his head on the way to the shower. His head hurt; his body hurt; his chest pulsed. What was going on? He stepped into the hot water and allowed it to awaken him. Then without shaving, he threw on his jeans, boots, and a black sweater. With a last quick glance at his weary face, he opened the door to his hotel room and exhaled.

The elevator doors opened and Jimmy stared into the lobby, trying to find his dad before his dad saw him. He wanted, in some small, victorious way, to be the first to recognize the other.

The man stood thin and alone, leaning against the wall next to the fireplace as if the floral wallpaper held him up. Wagner Sullivan stared toward the other bank of elevators, his face furrowed and tight, chewing his bottom lip while he rubbed his hands together. He wasn't the large man Jimmy remembered; time, memory, or liquor had shrunk him, or maybe it was some combination of all three that diminished this man he'd once called Dad.

Jimmy stepped forward and just watched him for a moment before he decided how to call his name. "Wagner," Jimmy said out loud.

Wagner turned, and his eyes filled with tears. Jimmy looked away from the pain. He would not be suckered into thinking this man cared about anything other than his next drink. Jimmy took three steps forward and held out his hand to shake.

Wagner looked down at Jimmy's hand with a sad smile. "No hug for the old man?"

Jimmy dropped his hand and shook his head. "You aren't my old man."

Wagner nodded. "Okay, fair enough. I figured you hated me, but hoped —"

"Well, don't hope anymore." Jimmy heard the callousness in his voice, but he couldn't stop the hate from rising. It was an ancient revulsion he'd thought long gone, but it arrived from the place of childhood, a land that really wasn't that far away at all.

Wagner cringed. "Can we sit down?" He motioned to a couch on their right.

Jimmy sat on the far end. "Okay, what are you doing here?"

"Well." Wagner sat and faced his son. "I

had this entire speech planned. But now I've forgotten the way it went."

Jimmy smelled the familiar aroma: whiskey. He felt the nausea of fear rise in his belly. This sweet-sour smell had meant only and always fighting, yelling, slammed doors. "You're drunk," Jimmy said.

"No." Wagner shook his head. "Maybe this would be easier if I were. I'm sober and have been for years. Listen, Jimmy. I know you must hate me. I know that. But just let me say a few things, okay?"

Jimmy nodded. "As long as you know I don't have anything to say to you."

"I know that."

Jimmy stared at this man and saw all that was gone — the bravado, the anger. And yet he saw what remained — the alcohol.

Wagner took in a long breath and leaned back onto the couch cushions. "I have one chance to say this, so I'll do my best. I love you, Jimmy. I love Jack. I always have."

"Yep, beating us was a great way to show that."

"I am here to say sorry. To apologize. The liquor ate me alive. It ate us alive. It killed me inside, and when that inside part was dead, I did things that a real man never would have done. I don't know when it happened or how it happened, but one day I was a man with a family and a wife and two brilliant sons and the next I was facedown in the street while your mother drove all of you into the dawn light and out of my life. It's not that I blame the liquor; I just blame myself for becoming the liquor." Wagner looked away and covered his face with one hand.

Jimmy nodded because an unbidden lump rising in the back of his throat would not allow words.

Wagner composed himself and faced Jimmy. "I live here in the city. I have for ten years now. When your mama took y'all away, I hit the road. I wandered for years. I tried to find you, but your mama did a good job of making sure I couldn't. I ended up here and somehow found myself in a rehab facility that was more like a dungeon, but I did get clean." He turned away. "I'm the janitor for a church on Fiftieth Street. I live in an apartment at the bottom of the church. It's not much of a life, but it's a sober life." Wagner paused and shifted his gaze to his lap where his hands were knit together.

Jimmy shook his head. "How did you find me?"

"I lost track for years, but then you and your band started showing up in my internet searches on the library computer, so I've been following you. When I read about your hit song and saw that you'd be in New York . . . I called all the fancy hotels near Rockefeller until I found you." He coughed and cleared his throat. "You look great, son. Please, although I know I don't have the right, please tell me how you're doing. Tell me about Jack." Wagner's face shook as he fought the tears that already sat in the corners of his eyes.

Jimmy took in all the details of his dad's face, and sorrow swelled next to the anger and whispered, *Have mercy.*

In a quick summary, Jimmy told his dad all the places they had lived. "Mama is in California. If you've been following the band, then you know what we've been up to. We're fine. Jack is in Ireland right now. He's getting married tomorrow. I'm here for a performance at Radio City, and then I'm flying to meet him. We've been living off the bus for a while now, but Jack and Kara will live in Seaboro."

"He went back to Seaboro to find her?"

"Well, actually, Kara found him."

"He's marrying the girl next door. Wow." Wagner smiled for the first time. "And that song of yours. It seems to have brought you to me finally."

"That's not what the song is about —

176

bringing me to you."

"What *is* the song about?" his dad asked quietly.

"Love. It's a love song."

Wagner nodded, and his eyes glistened with unshed tears. "Yes. I know. Well, I promised I'd only bother you for five minutes, and it's been more than that. I don't want to break another promise to you. I just needed to see your face, to tell you I never stopped loving you and that I'm sorrier than any man could be. Even when I was lost, you and Jack have always been on my mind. Always. Every day. Please tell Jack." Now the man did begin to cry, large tears rolling down his wrinkled cheeks as he stood. "I can't buy a ticket to hear you tonight, but I'll be outside in case I can hear something . . ."

Jimmy stood to face the man. "Why did you come here, Wagner?"

"I just told you." He didn't reach to wipe away a single tear, allowing them to settle in the wrinkles of his face.

"No, really. Why? The real reason. Do you want forgiveness? Did you expect me to invite you to the concert? Did you want to see Jack? Do you need money?"

Wagner shook his head. "No. I came to tell you that I'm proud of you. I came because I love you. I'm not the man I ever wanted to be, but that doesn't change the way I feel about you or your brother. That is why I came. That's all." Wagner looked, for the first time in twenty years, directly into his son's eyes. "I am sorry. I love you."

With the words Jimmy had wanted to hear all his life, Wagner turned and walked away.

Jimmy watched the slim, broken figure as his dad pushed open the double doors and then glanced back with a smile. A sad smile. Wagner disappeared into the outside crowd, and Jimmy stood in the lobby for a full five minutes before he began to shake with emotions he couldn't name. The whiskey aroma remained, and Jimmy realized, in a moment of gut-dropping recognition, that it was *not* his dad he'd smelled, but his own breath. His own sweat and his own life — an apparition showing Jimmy who he was becoming.

Jimmy returned, trembling, to his hotel room. He rushed into the bathroom and splashed his face with cold water, then glanced into the mirror at his haggard face, one that seemed to reflect many images: who he wanted to be and who he was becoming. Why was he here when those he loved were in Ireland?

The song.

He leaned closer to the mirror and wiped at his image. The song. Yes. He was here for the song and what it could do for him and for Charlotte, and for the band.

What is the song really about? his mind asked in a voice clear and loud.

Unexpected love.

Long-awaited love.

Redemptive love that heals and helps one to begin again.

Love born of innocence.

Christmas, exactly.

Jimmy had always hoped his dad knew about him, was proud of him. But if that was all he ever wanted, why did he still feel empty and hollowed out?

He didn't write the song for his dad's return. He wrote for the feeling they all waited for when the strings of the guitar were plucked: inspiration. The thrill of tapping into something bigger than himself. The energy that came when they hit on a truth that couldn't be told in any other way but the song they'd just written. And that was what had happened with Charlotte.

He ate a room service breakfast of stale croissants and jelly, cold scrambled eggs, and bacon in silence and decided that a long, cold walk would clear his head. He threw on his coat, and by the time he stood on the corner of Fifth Avenue and Fifty-Second Street, he was overcome with the need to talk to Jack. He pulled out his phone and called his brother. But there was no answer. It was 6:00 p.m. in Ireland, and they would all be at the rehearsal or the dinner celebration where Jimmy was supposed to be the best man and make a toast.

Jimmy finally decided to look at the photo Jack had sent the night before and stood in the freezing cold, shivering, waiting for the picture to load. Then he stared at Jack, Kara, Charlotte, and a dark-haired Irishman dancing in front of a band. Charlotte's head was back, and he knew her look of laughter.

Regret snuck up behind him and grabbed him around the middle where his ribs contracted; he released a groan. What was he doing here? If proving himself were the point, if measuring up and success were the point, then the man who just came to his hotel would have been enough. Would anything *ever* be enough? Only, as he'd written in his song, only love was enough.

He stared again at the phone. He was missing his brother's wedding. He might have lost Charlotte. All in the name of what? Not love.

His song with Charlotte had become

something else altogether. He'd taken a beautiful creation and allowed the world to twist it into something he never meant it to be.

His mind began to flick rapidly through the options. He could leave for Ireland right now and get there on time, but he'd maxed out his credit card waiting for the final paycheck. He tapped his phone and called the airline to find the next flight.

The airline employee's voice was flat and lifeless. "Yes, there is only one flight today, and it leaves in two hours and six minutes."

"How much would it be to change my ticket from tomorrow to today?" Jimmy placed his hand over the phone to keep the wind from distorting his voice.

The employee continued with all the vital information in the most unvital voice. His big check would come next week, and until then Milton had given him cash spending money. He hadn't needed anything, as the tour had supplied everything. Until now. He had two hours to make an international flight and figure out how to pay for a ticket.

Impossible.

"Can't I just transfer my ticket? I don't have that kind of money."

"Then I don't know how to help you." The robotic voice held no compassion.

Jimmy hung up and groaned.

The crowd pushed him toward the wall where a woman who looked to be homeless was wearing a thick, white down jacket that covered her from neck to feet. Over the jacket were pinned tattered, dirty angel wings made of muddy feather boas. She smiled at Jimmy and he looked away, avoiding being asked for a handout. A drunken man jostled into Jimmy, shoving him into the angel. "Sorry," Jimmy mumbled to the angel.

"It's no problem. But you look mighty miserable. You okay there, son?"

He stared at this old woman, whose lilting voice did not match her cragged face and dirty clothes. "Yeah, I'm fine. Thank you."

She smiled and moved away from a pawnshop, its lights neon and flashing with a red arrow pointing toward the front door.

A pawnshop.

He stepped in with his hand in his pocket where he'd been carrying Charlotte's ring for days now.

Jimmy glanced again at the woman who had, in an odd way, shown him the answer to his question — how would he get the money for a change in ticket? The Claddagh engagement ring. He could come back after Ireland and buy her ring back, but all that mattered now was getting on that flight that left in two hours.

He entered the dimly lit store, pulling a small box from his pocket.

It was Christmas Eve twilight, and the group in Ireland, which now included Kara's sister, Deidre, and her husband, Bill, along with her brother, Brian, who had landed only hours ago, stood in front of the church waiting for the church director to meet them for the rehearsal. They'd all scattered during the day, some touring Galway, others resting and reading. Charlotte and Kara had wandered the streets, alleyways, and museums of Galway where Kara took photos of Christmas lights for her new portfolio. They tried to find the places Maeve had spoken about, walk the paths she had walked, take photos of her land and time. They visited the jewelry store, which was purported to have made the original Claddagh ring. Kara had asked to meet the owner but was told she was out of town and would return in the morning.

Deidre shivered in her down jacket. "This is beautiful, Kara. Simply amazing."

Charlotte entered the church first and the others followed. She winked at the Mary statue, glancing down to see the shell still resting as an offering.

They went through the wedding motions with the church coordinator, Iona. When they stood at the altar, each in their place, Iona, in her soft Irish accent, asked Kara, "Would you like me to place the leaves tonight? I think our congregation would love to see them, to know they came from where Maeve lived the last of her life."

"What leaves?" Jack asked.

Kara smiled. "I have a surprise for you." Then she looked to Iona. "If you'll tell me where they are, I'll get them."

Iona held up her hand. "They are back in the sacristy. They came last night. I haven't unpacked them."

Kara followed Iona, and when she returned she held a single magnolia leaf in her hand. She walked toward Jack, who leaned against a pew. "This," she said with a sweet smile on her face, "is from the very tree where we used to hide when we were kids. My dad recruited the ladies in the neighborhood to gather enough to put them on each pew end."

Jack, who had held it together quite nicely until this moment, fought the tears rising in his throat and eyes. "Kara," he said in a tender, quiet voice. "I am the luckiest man in the world."

She kissed him right there in that church in front of family, friends, and Iona, in front of God and Our Lady of Galway and St. Thomas Aquinas.

Jimmy Sullivan sold the ring for half of what he'd bought it for, but it was enough cash to get a ticket to Ireland if and only if he arrived at the airport in time. He ran outside to hail a cab. The Christmas Eve crowd pushed into stores, hotels, and high-rises. He stood at the curb and felt the plop of cold snow fall onto his hand, a teardrop landing on his cell phone screen. He glanced up. The flakes were large, tumbling onto and over one another, white obscuring and filling the sky, gathering strength.

"No," he mumbled and shoved his phone into his pocket. He noticed another cab approaching and flagged it down, and when it stopped he moved toward the back door.

A woman in all black jumped out of the back seat, and the cabbie yelled toward Jimmy, "Off duty."

Jimmy leaned down and spoke into the open window. "I'm desperate. I need to get to the airport for a plane that leaves in less than two hours."

The cabbie didn't answer but drove away, leaving Jimmy jumping back onto the sidewalk where he bumped into a young girl. Her face was surrounded by a bright-yellow plastic, or maybe it was foam, star. Either way, her head had been transformed into the celestial body that guided the wise men to the stable. "I'm sorry," he said and bent over to look into her bluest eyes.

"That's okay." The little girl spoke while gazing directly at Jimmy. "We're late too."

A woman bundled up in a black fur coat glared at Jimmy. "Excuse me," she said and grabbed the little girl's hand, pulling her toward a long, black limousine.

"Wait, Mother," she said and walked toward Jimmy. "Will you miss your plane?"

Jimmy nodded; she must have heard him begging the cabbie. "If I don't get a cab, I will."

"Where are you going?"

Jimmy smiled at her star-face. "Ireland."

"That far away?"

"Yes," he said, enchanted with the flecks of light and dark playing in her eyes. Snow fell harder now, landing on her eyelashes and black parka. "That far away."

"You want to spend Christmas with someone you love." Her voice was clear as the bells of a church ringing.

He smiled at her. "Where are you going all dressed up like a star?"

"I'm the guiding light in the Christmas Eve pageant tonight. I really don't do anything but stand there, but I guess I'm still important. The shepherds won't get there without me."

He smiled and almost patted her on the head, but thought better of it with her mother's stern look. "Go be a star. Your mom's waiting."

"You won't get there without me either," the little girl said in a quiet voice.

"Pardon?" Jimmy asked.

"Mother," the girl said and turned to the woman. "This man has to get to the airport right now or he will spend Christmas all alone."

"Dear, I'm quite sure that man knows how to get a cab."

The little girl didn't flinch but stood firm. Was he really willing to stand there and have a little girl beg for him? He turned to leave.

"Come back," the little girl said sternly, in a voice grown-up and firm.

Jimmy stopped.

"No," the woman in the black coat said. "We can't, Maria. We can't save the entire world. You've got to stop this."

"It's not the whole world. It's one man. Imagine, Mother, if you were alone tonight and stuck somewhere. Roger will just be sitting there waiting for us in the car. Why can't he take this sad man to the airport?"

The woman looked at Jimmy, and her face held so many conflicting emotions, Jimmy couldn't decide whether she was mad, sad, or irritated with her young daughter. Then she took in a deep breath. "I'm sorry," she said to Jimmy. "I didn't mean to be rude. The holidays, they kill me. I don't think this is the way it's supposed to be. If you can spare another five minutes, our driver will drop us off, and then I'll tell him to take you to the airport while Maria is in her play. She's right. He'll have time."

"Ma'am," Jimmy said, "that is too generous. I can't accept."

"Yes, you can. Consider it a Christmas present. Now, don't stand here and talk me out of it. We're late, and so are you."

"Thank you," Jimmy said, "You have no idea . . ." And then his voice broke as he crawled into the back seat of the limousine as the woman explained the situation to the driver.

Roger, the driver, looked back to Jimmy. "I recognize you, man. You're that country singer who was on TV last week. You seriously want to make an international flight that leaves in less than two hours?"

"Yes," Jimmy said.

"That'll take a miracle, but I'll do my best."

12

What fills the eyes fills the heart.
— OLD IRISH PROVERB

The lights strung around the room twinkled like stars hung for Kara and Jack. Although Charlotte knew they'd been hung for Christmas, tonight it felt as if everything was set for love's forever promise. The restaurant was filled with families and patrons while the Larson-Sullivan wedding party gathered at one long table in the back.

Charlotte stood and lifted her champagne glass. "Okay, as the maid of honor, I make the toast."

Everyone raised their Waterford flute and Charlotte looked over at Kara and Jack. "Here's to Maeve Mahoney and her story, to the story that brought you together."

"Hear, hear," echoed across the table.

"And to Kara, for recognizing the truth inside the story," Charlotte said and blew a kiss down the table.

It was time for the best man to make his toast, and his absence was a void. Finally, Brian stood. "My turn." He looked to Charlotte and smiled and then turned to his sister. "I would not and could not have picked a better brother if I'd tried. Welcome to the family."

Brian said more, but Charlotte could not stop her mind from wandering to Jimmy. This was the part where he would have read that speech he'd worked on for days. This was the part where he'd sit next to Charlotte and hold her hand and whisper that he loved her. This was the part . . .

Charlotte stopped her thoughts from going any further because in truth, this was the part where she missed him and her heart broke for all that could have been and was not. She turned her eyes and concentration back to Jack and Kara, lifted her champagne, and took a long swallow.

Brian leaned close to her. "You okay?"

Charlotte nodded. "Jack's brother should be here for him. I want to be mad at Jimmy, but I can't." Quick tears flashed in her eyes. "I keep trying to work myself into anger . . ."

"Crazy thing love is," Brian said and shook his head. "I'm trying to stay away from it." He lifted his champagne and clinked his glass with hers.

Charlotte smiled at him. "Good luck with that."

The snow in New York City fell in clumps, hitting the limousine windshield and melting on impact. Jimmy glanced at his cell, saw the battery level was low, and dialed Milton's number. His stomach dropped in dread; he knew this was not going to end well.

"Hey, man," Milton answered. "Your courier is only an hour away from the hotel. This snow is screwing everything up. I'm sorry. They will pick up your guitar and luggage in time for the performance. No worries."

Jimmy exhaled, closed his eyes. "I'm not worried, Milton, because I'm not there. I'm on my way to the airport. I never should have agreed to miss my brother's wedding."

"Please tell me you're kidding. Please tell me you're sitting in the hotel room. Please."

"Sorry." Jimmy cringed at the word. "Listen, there is only one thing I can control, and that is the songwriting. What it has become and what others do with it are not in my power. I am going to see my family."

"Turn around. Now. There is no way I am

192

telling Radio City to take you off the schedule. No way. This is my reputation, Steele."

"And this is my family, Milton. The only family I have. And my name is Jimmy."

Milton's colorful response echoed loudly and Jimmy saw the driver's wry smile. Jimmy hung up and leaned his head against the window. The traffic on the Belt Parkway crawled at less than ten miles an hour, and Jimmy leaned forward to Roger. "We gonna make it?"

"I don't think so. I'm trying."

Jimmy settled back against the seat. Time took on another dimension, one in which every minute meant a change in his destiny, an alteration in all that was important, and there he sat, without any control.

Slowly they inched toward JFK, and with just under an hour until takeoff, they finally pulled to the curb at check-in. Jimmy thanked Roger and took his card so he could send him a tip. Roger smiled. "It was my pleasure. Better than sitting and waiting. I hope you make it."

"Me too." Jimmy ran toward the doors, flinging his backpack over his shoulder. He stopped short when he entered the lobby. A line snaked through the makeshift lanes — hundreds of people. He quickly scanned the crowd and found an airline employee.

"Excuse me." Jimmy stopped the employee, noticed the name Joseph on his name tag. "Excuse me, but I'm trying to make a flight that leaves in less than an hour, and that line looks like it's going to take at least twice that."

The man laughed. "Ain't no way, buddy. Sorry."

"Listen," Jimmy said. "This is sort of an emergency."

"It always is."

Jimmy closed his eyes to regain his composure, and his soul sent forth the most fervent wish, the most desperate hope to see Charlotte, to see Jack, to be in Ireland before the wedding. Then he ran after Joseph. "Please. I'm supposed to be in Ireland for my brother's wedding and —"

Joseph looked at Jimmy and shook his head. "International travel requires you to be here at least two hours before departure."

"I know. But I also know that the flight I need to be on is sitting at the gate and I don't have any luggage. It's Christmas Eve. Come on, can you help me out? What would you do if you were in my situation, needing to see your family?"

Joseph stood still for a moment, looked over Jimmy's head, and said, "I'd give anything to be with my family tonight. Guess I could at least help *you* do that."

Jimmy's smile could not have been more authentic.

"Come with me. I'm not sure we can do this, but we'll try."

Jimmy followed the man to a counter.

"No promises." Joseph clicked on a computer, began to punch in numbers. "Your ticket?" He held his hand out.

Jimmy cringed. "Well, see, there's a problem there too. I have a ticket for tomorrow, and I know there's a huge change fee. But I have the cash."

Joseph looked up at him, shaking his head. "You just trying to make this as difficult as possible?" But he had a smile on his face, and Jimmy handed him the ticket and the cash. While Joseph worked on the ticket, Jimmy counted his money. There might be just enough for a rental car. He'd figure that part out when he landed in Ireland.

After what seemed like an eternity of button punching, Joseph looked up with a grin of satisfaction. "You aren't going to believe this. There is one more seat, and the plane is delayed due to weather. Deicing takes time. Planes are backed up." He handed a ticket to Jimmy. "Crazy."

The relief that spread through Jimmy

made him dizzy. "Merry Christmas, Joe. I wish you the most merry Christmas you've ever had."

"You too." Joseph's smile proved, once again, that giving offers as much or more to the giver as to the receiver.

Waiting at the gate, Jimmy dialed Jack's number, calculating that they were all in the middle of the rehearsal dinner. No one answered, and Jimmy settled back into the plastic seat, staring at the overhead screen for updates on flight departure. He decided not to leave a message. What if the plane didn't leave on time, or at all? He held his ticket and wished for a hot shower, for his luggage with his chargers and toothbrush. He'd roll into Ireland looking like a disheveled vagabond. But then again, better to show up as he was and always had been than to not show up at all.

He turned off his phone to preserve the battery. Time crept on as Jimmy thought of the events of the past several hours: leaving his luggage and guitar in New York City; canceling a performance at Radio City; selling the ring he'd meant for a romantic proposal. He didn't have his suit or any clothing other than what he wore, and now the flight might not even leave before nightfall.

He calculated the losses as an accountant would write numbers in the debit column. Then he moved his thoughts to where he was going — not what he was leaving. He calmed himself thinking he was going toward all that mattered, and he let go of everything else.

13

'Tis afterwards that everything
is understood.
— OLD IRISH PROVERB

Charlotte awoke at midnight, the stars so
close they seemed to fall from the sky,
through the window, and into her hotel
room. Kara slept soundly in the next bed
and Charlotte thought of the line between
married and single, between love and hate,
between forgiveness and forgetting. Sometimes there isn't a line; there is just the lifting of fog or the accumulation of time and
knowing. But in getting married there is a
moment, a definite *before* and a firm *after.*

She grabbed her pen and notebook from
the bag on the floor and settled against the
headboard. Her mind spun with jet lag and
emotion, and she searched for the split in
time when she fell in love. When she
couldn't find the words, she closed her eyes

and imagined Jimmy. It was midnight in New York, and he'd either just be finishing or doing the finale. And as Kara stirred awake, Charlotte sent Jimmy love and peace on this Christmas Day, Kara's wedding day.

The plane from JFK took off for Shannon four hours late. Passengers were irritable and hungry; children were whining and women grumbling. The flight attendants handed out free drinks and consoled the passengers with the truth that it was better to be safe than on time.

Jimmy settled back into his window seat at the very rear of the plane, directly against the back wall of the toilets. "Lucky me," he mumbled, then remembered that yes, he was lucky. This was the last seat.

The plane full and in flight, Jimmy tried to sleep in a perfectly upright position with an older woman next to him reading with her light on. He finally gave up and leafed through the airline magazine to choose a movie.

"Aye," the woman next to him mumbled.

"Excuse me?" Jimmy asked.

She looked at him, and for the first time he noticed that her eyes were the most brilliant green he'd ever seen. He smiled.

"Did I speak out loud?" she asked in an

Irish accent.

"Yes, but it's okay."

"I was hoping for a movie I wanted to see, but they are all . . . inane. This flight is so long and after all that waiting in the airport. Now I'll barely make it home to spend Christmas morning with my family."

"Do you live in Ireland?" Jimmy asked, thankful for the distraction of someone else's life.

"I do. I was here visiting my son and grandchildren. But that's what I get for trying to be in two places at once for Christmas."

"I know what you mean."

"Why are you visiting our fair isle?"

"My brother. His wedding is tomorrow." Jimmy paused, calculating. "For him it's today, because in Ireland it's Christmas morning. His wedding morning."

"Ah," she said. "And here we are, suspended in the sky."

"Exactly."

"By the way, my name is Elaine O'Brien."

"I'm Jimmy Sullivan. Nice to meet you." He grinned at her and felt some of the stress melt.

She patted his arm like a mother might. "Is your entire family already there?"

There was something in her eyes, in the

lilt and flow of her speech and smile, that caused Jimmy to tell this old woman his *entire* story — to narrate the tale of the song and how he wrote it with Charlotte. He told her about the Claddagh ring, the tour, the concert, and his dad. In an unspooling of the past months, Mrs. O'Brien learned about all that had happened to Jimmy until now, when he sat on that plane trying to get to his brother's wedding and to the woman he loved.

The morning arrived crisp and cold, and the swans appeared to be dressed for the wedding. The women gathered in Kara and Charlotte's room, wishing each other Merry Christmas and taking turns using the mirror to put on their makeup. Kara's hair was pinned back with loose curls falling, her mother's veil in her hand.

Kara tilted her head back to let Rosie attach the veil. "When I imagined my wedding day as a child, I don't think I ever imagined us all cramped into a teeny hotel room sharing a single mirror on Christmas Day. But what I did imagine was that my mom would be here." Her voice caught and she looked heavenward. "But in many ways she is here."

Rosie hugged Kara from behind. "We love

201

you so."

"Yes, we do. And I've been thinking of your mom too. I bet she's watching and loving every moment of this." Charlotte smiled at her best friend and then turned to her mother. "Can you zip me?"

Rosie zipped up the dress and kissed her daughter's cheek. She whispered in her ear, "Darling, are you doing okay?"

Charlotte nodded. "I am. I promise. Today is for Kara."

Rosie clapped her hands together once. "Okay, I don't want to be bossy, but we need to walk over to the church. It's time."

Bundled in scarves and coats, the women were like a bouquet of wildflowers tumbling out of the hotel and walking two blocks to the church. The morning was clear, the sky swept of stars and clouds, of anything at all but the sun hanging on the far horizon. The bay shivered beneath the cold, exposed to the sky without protection. The swans flapped and danced, teasing one another and the shoreline. The Christmas lights, strung from trees and light posts, winked even in daylight, as though they knew where the women were going and what they were doing.

Once inside the church, Iona took their coats. "The first Christmas mass is finished, and there is one in progress now. And then the wedding. Are you ready?"

Kara nodded. "Ready as I've ever been."

"You're a beautiful bride," Iona said and smiled. "Radiant."

"Thanks. Are the guys here yet?"

Iona smiled. "Yes, they're waiting in the back room, telling jokes I do not want to hear." She smiled. "All is well, I promise. Let me escort you to the bride's room, and I'll be back in about thirty minutes to take you into the sacristy."

Charlotte stepped forward. "Do you mind," she asked both Iona and Kara, "if I walk around to the entryway for a couple minutes?"

"Of course not," Kara said.

Charlotte wanted to see Our Lady of Galway one more time. She wanted to touch the hem of her wooden skirt and see her expression of peace, her countenance that seemed to say all would be well. Yes, all will be well.

Jimmy stood at the rental car desk ringing the call bell for an employee. When the plane had landed he'd attempted to turn on his cell phone, only to find he had no service in Ireland — which was probably a good thing, because then he couldn't listen to the ten ranting voice mails from Milton. Finally, a young girl with purple hair and a nose ring came through a back door into the overheated office.

"Merry Christmas," Jimmy said, glancing at his watch while digging into his pocket. "I need a car and a map to the Claddagh Village." He paused after hearing his rough tone. "Please."

The girl ambled toward the computer. "I don't think we have any cars left. It's Christmas."

Jimmy groaned. The wedding would begin in an hour and a half and the drive was almost exactly that. "Anything. I'll drive anything," he said.

She squinted at the screen. "Although you'd be saying you'd drive anything, like I told ya, there's nothing."

"There must be. Just one car. Just one."

She laughed. "Only my clunker, and you won't be wanting to drive that." Her sweet Irish accent made the word *clunker* sound like a good thing.

Jimmy leaned forward on the desk. "Okay, here's the deal. My brother's wedding starts in an hour and a half. I've gone through hell to get here. I left my luggage in New York, sat next to the airplane bathroom in a straight-up position for eight hours, and

204

now a car is all that's left between me and my brother's wedding."

Her eyes opened wide. "Really? Is all that true?"

He laughed. "Unfortunately, yes." He held out his cash. "I can give this to you, along with a promise of utmost sincerity that I will bring the car back as soon as the wedding is over."

"Hey," she said. "Why don't I drive you? You can pay me to drive and then you won't have to return the car. I was on the night shift and I'm off now. I need an excuse to be late. My da is home for the holidays. What do you say?"

"Let's go." Jimmy smiled.

The purple-haired girl, whose name was Lydia, drove them through the crisp Christmas morning, around the curves of road and past green meadows and the breathtaking bay.

"So, can you be telling me why your brother is getting married in Ireland, and of all places, a little fishing village?"

"It's a complicated story, but it all has to do with this old lady who told his fiancée a story."

"What kind of story?"

"About the Claddagh ring and about her life."

Lydia smiled and tapped her steering wheel. "Tell me."

Jack laughed. "You people and stories."

"That's our thing." She kept her eyes on the road but grinned widely.

"Well, this woman, Maeve Mahoney, was in a nursing home and —"

Lydia slammed on her brakes, pulled to the side of the road.

"What's wrong?" Jimmy pointed to the road.

"Say the name again."

He did.

She laughed with a sound that was more of a song than it was anything else. "She was my great-gram."

Jimmy shook his head. "This is just getting weirder and weirder."

Lydia pulled the car back onto the road. "Okay, I'll get you there, but you have to finish the story."

And so he did.

Lydia drove down the Claddagh Quay, then pointed.

"That's the church there."

Jimmy stared at the granite structure in the morning sun, the beauty of it mirrored in the bay, making it appear that there were two churches, one of permanence and one of a dream world. He glanced at his watch and then at Lydia.

"The wedding started five minutes ago."

She stopped the car. "Well, then you better hurry."

Jimmy took that moment to look into her eyes. "I don't know how to thank you, but I will find a way."

"Ah, Great-Grandmam would tell me it was my privilege."

Jimmy threw open the car door and bolted for the front of the church. He entered with the wind behind his back, the cold forcing its way in. His sneakers squeaked on the marble, and he found himself face-to-face with Our Lady of Galway. Her presence caused him to pause and he touched her hand, feeling he knew her or had met her before. Then he lifted his gaze and opened the wooden doors to the sanctuary.

There they stood — Kara and Jack, facing each other, Charlotte standing at Kara's side, and Mr. Larson where he, Jimmy, should be. Jimmy took his first step down the aisle, moving slowly. Should he head toward the altar or slip into a pew?

Charlotte was the first to see him and she took in a sharp breath, her eyes opening wider before she reached out and touched Kara's elbow. Kara turned to her maid of honor, who lifted her chin and gaze toward Jimmy. Kara and Jack spun around, and the priest stopped speaking, his mouth open. Jimmy offered a timid wave and stopped midaisle waiting for someone to tell him what to do. Sit? Run? Approach the altar?

Kara nodded at Jack. "Go to him."

Jack and Jimmy met halfway in that rose and magnolia–adorned aisle, and Jimmy spoke first. "I'm sorry. I am so, so sorry."

Jack placed his hands on Jimmy's shoulders and stared into his eyes. "Merry Christmas, brother." And he hugged him with a hearty laugh. "Come join the ceremony."

When Jimmy reached Kara, he kissed her cheek. "I'm sorry." Then he turned to Charlotte with the hope of any man who turns to the woman he loves. She smiled at him, bit her bottom lip to stop her tears. Jimmy smiled and took his place as best man. The words — they would come later.

In the vestibule, Our Lady of Galway watched the small gathering of Mr. and Mrs. Jack Sullivan and their friends and family. Kara had lifted her veil and she held her husband's hand. Jimmy Sullivan stood in front of his brother and his friends and family and apologized once again.

Jack held up his hand to stop the apologies. "You're here, and that is all that matters."

Jimmy shook his head. "Look at me. I probably messed up your nice wedding photographs in my jeans and boots." He motioned toward the photographer, who was snapping pictures of Charlotte, Deidre, and Rosie.

"I don't believe you've messed up anything, big brother. Except maybe . . ." Jack motioned toward Charlotte with a nod of his head.

Jimmy approached Charlotte, and together they stood in front of Our Lady. A hush fell over the vestibule. "Charlotte Lynn Carrington, I have never loved as I have loved you. I'm sorry I wasn't here. I'm sorry I lost sight of all I know about you and our love."

"That song was ours," she told him, her voice quivering, "and you gave it away. You let the world change it and you."

"The song will always be ours. I shared it with the world and it was almost lost, but both the song and our love brought me back to you." He dropped to one knee. "You awoke love in me. You awoke the song in me. I do and always will belong to you. Say you'll be my wife. Please?"

Charlotte didn't answer but instead held

out her hand for him to take. When he did, she drew him to stand so they faced each other. Jimmy's pulse throbbed in his throat and chest — was she finally done with him?

She kissed his hand and then spoke quietly. "Yes, Jimmy Sullivan. A million yeses."

He kissed her gently, and before anyone could clap or rejoice, he said, "I bought you a ring, but I sold it to get on the flight. At this moment all I have to give you is my heart and a promise."

"That," Charlotte said, "is all I ever wanted." She placed her head on his shoulder and he pulled her to him, wrapped his arms around her, and held her as close as a man can hold a woman.

The small crowd clapped and whooped and made noises that at any other time would seem inappropriate in the church. Then cold air rushed in as the double doors opened, and an older woman bundled in a puffy down coat and knit hat entered and glanced around the vestibule until her green eyes lit like lanterns. "Mr. Sullivan?"

They all stopped and stared at what seemed an apparition.

"Mrs. O'Brien. What are you doing here?"

"I never did tell you that I'm the Mrs. O'Brien of the Claddagh Jeweler, the original Claddagh ring maker here in Galway."

Jimmy laughed with a fullness he hadn't felt in months. "I guess I shouldn't be surprised."

"And where is this Charlotte?"

Charlotte stepped forward, brushing the tears from her eyes. "Here."

The woman held her hand out to Jimmy and slipped something into his palm. "Now, do it right this time, son. This is a symbol of faith, friendship, and love. Offer it in that spirit." And she turned with a grin and disappeared as quickly as she'd appeared.

By the time Jimmy saw the Claddagh ring with the large emerald in the middle, Mrs. O'Brien was gone. He turned to Charlotte, overwhelmed with the realization that sometimes hope is not only fulfilled but filled to overflowing. Now he knew better than to turn away a gift of such grace. He slipped the ring on Charlotte's finger.

When the hugging and tears subsided, Jack shook his head and asked Jimmy, "How did you get here? What happened?"

"It was crazy, really." Jimmy looked around the foyer. "First Dad showed up." He looked at Jack. "More on that later. And then there was a homeless angel and a child named Maria dressed like a guiding star and then a guy named Joseph who got me on the flight. And then Maeve's great-granddaughter drove me to the church." He shook his head. "And here I am."

Kara laughed and took Charlotte's hand. "An angel. A star. A Joseph and a Claddagh ring. You'd think Maeve Mahoney had something to do with this, wouldn't you?"

The pub was full of villagers and the night was in full swing as the wedding party joined a local Christmas gathering in the town center. Since the couple was obvious in their wedding attire, the town congratulated, lifted glasses, and bought rounds of drinks for all. The word spread quickly about Mrs. O'Brien and the ring, and Jimmy and Charlotte posed for photos with everyone who asked.

"Should we call you Steele now?" Isabelle asked with a laugh, elbowing Jimmy as he made his way to the bar.

"Never." He pulled her into a hug. "I missed y'all so badly."

A few feet away, on a bench at a corner table, Kara and Charlotte admired the people they loved, basked in the glory of it all. Isabelle danced to the Celtic music with a dark-haired local; Deidre and Bill sat at the bar pretending to learn Irish accents while Mr. Larson laughed until his face turned red. Kara twisted in her seat. "I have to tell you something, Charlotte. Please don't be mad at me. I did it because I love you."

"What did you do?" Charlotte leaned back and took in Kara's features in an attempt to figure out if she was serious.

Kara cringed and removed her phone from her purse and turned it on, opened her email, and handed it to Charlotte. "Read this."

While Charlotte read the email, her green silk dress hem becoming sticky on the pub floor, Jimmy arrived and slid in next to her, wrapped his arm around her. "What's that?"

Charlotte didn't look, but continued reading. "Kara's phone."

Jimmy leaned forward and glanced at Kara. "Huh?"

"It's an email," Kara said. "Our Charlotte has sold a song to Faith Hill."

Jimmy rubbed his forehead in confusion, and Charlotte held up Kara's phone. "You sent my work out without telling me?"

"That's what you want to say when Faith just bought your lyrics?" Kara made a face. "I'm sorry. I know it was wrong, but I read them when you left me alone at the house that afternoon, and they were the most beautiful lyrics I'd ever read. I've seen enough songwriters' work to know it was better than you had any idea. So I took a quick photo of two of your poems and asked Jack to mail them to his agent and . . . now this."

"Jack knew too?" Charlotte's chest started to constrict and she grasped Jimmy's hand. "Those aren't lyrics, Kara. Those are poems. Really personal poems about how I was feeling with Jimmy so far gone from me. They were personal poems about trying to find my way in the dark while everyone else was all cheery-holiday-happy."

"*And* they are beautiful words."

Jimmy pulled her close. "Charlotte, love. You sold the rights to Faith Hill. Did you hear her? My talented, beautiful girl. You did that."

"I don't understand." Charlotte thought about her poems being passed around, of her emotions being scrutinized and evaluated. "You should have told me, Kara. You should have asked." Charlotte moved away from her friend, sliding on the bench.

"I know. I should have. But you would have said no, and, Charlotte, you can't hide that light of yours. It is *too* bright. The world can heal with your words. You can help someone else." She reached out her hand. "Don't be angry."

Charlotte stood, wanting to run, but worried that she might destroy the fragile reconciliation she had just found with Jimmy. Then she glanced between Kara and Jimmy and sat again. "I don't know . . ." She looked to the man she loved. "All this time I've been blaming the music, believing the music took you away from me." She looked to Kara. "That's why I didn't want to show them to anyone. I thought it would make things worse, that anything to do with sharing my words with the music world would destroy us. I didn't want anyone to know how I felt. But it's not true, is it? The music didn't take you away." She returned her attention to Jimmy. "And it didn't ruin anything. Our song brought you back to me."

"Yes," Jimmy said carefully. "Remember on the porch when we wrote the song?"

Charlotte nodded as tears gathered.

"That night," Jimmy said softly, "you said that music saves us, and you were right."

He kissed her just as the lead singer, a lanky man with dark hair and a Scottish accent, shouted into the audience, "I hear we have celebrities in the house. There are some requests to bring them to the stage."

Jimmy held on to Charlotte. "I think I'll let Jack take this."

"No." She shook her head. "No hiding our light." She winked.

215

Jack's and Jimmy's eyes found each other in the crowd and they both shook their heads. "No way," Jack hollered and waved off the request. "This is your gig."

The singer held out the microphone. "Come on, man, just one song. This lady over here won't leave us be until you sing."

Isabelle stood at the side of the stage with a satisfied grin.

Jack made his way to Jimmy's side as he stood. "You gave up performing on the biggest stage tonight. So let's sing here."

Jimmy glanced down at Charlotte and she nodded yes. Seeing defeat was sure, Jimmy ambled toward the stage and borrowed the guitar, fiddling with it for a moment before he stepped to the microphone with his brother and began to play the tune he'd been singing for weeks, the song he'd written with Charlotte, the song that had taken him from her and the song that had reminded him of all that was important — love.

When they finished, only the most cynical weren't moved. Jimmy jumped off the stage to the whoops and claps of the small crowd and came to Charlotte, throwing his arms around her. "That's ours. We made that together. And we'll make so much more."

"Jimmy, I didn't mean to write another

song. I was just trying to find my way through the confusion."

"A song, exactly."

Charlotte gazed at him and drew him closer. "I thought I lost you to the music and the road and the fame."

He shook his head. "No. All of that only matters if it brings me to you. Otherwise, it's all just noise."

The crowd pressed in around them as they held each other, dancing as Christmas night ended and love again found an unexpected way to change the world.

SHORTBREAD RECIPE

(A Steele family recipe from Patti's
grandmother, Bonnie Steele)

1 cup butter
1 cup sugar
4 cups flour

1. Heat oven to 275 degrees F.
2. Cream butter and sugar together until smooth.
3. Add flour and mix with hands.
4. Put in pan and flatten to approx. 1 inch.
5. Prick with fork in any pattern you please.
6. Bake for 1 hour or until light brown.
7. Cut while warm.

CHARLOTTE'S SOUTHERN GARLAND

Materials:
Evergreen trimmings
Twine
24-gauge floral wire
Your favorite added decorations (e.g., dried pomegranates, mercury ornaments, magnolia leaves, etc.)

1. Gather your evergreen trimmings. The more you gather, the longer and fuller the garland will be. (Charlotte spent hours wandering the backwoods of her mama's house, piling her wheelbarrow high and wide with juniper, pine, and magnolia.)
2. Gather the things you want to add to the evergreen. (Charlotte used dried pomegranates and mercury Christmas ornaments.) Choose whatever strikes your fancy and will

be a complement to your holiday design! Set these decorations aside.

3. Pile all your beautiful trimmings and begin to cut them into approximately six-inch pieces.

4. Cut a ten-foot length of twine. Lay this twine straight on a flat surface and then tie a loop into one end of it.

5. Pick up your 24-gauge floral wire and attach it to the loop. DON'T cut your wire yet — keep it on the spool so you can unwind the wire as you go along.

6. Gather a handful of evergreen trimmings and loop the floral wire around the ends of this bundle. Arrange the bunch with the stems facing the twine-loop and attach the evergreen to the twine by wrapping the floral wire around both the twine and the end of the bundle. Continue looping the wire around bundles of evergreen, bunching bundles as close together as possible. (Don't forget — the stems face the end with the loop where you started.)

7. Continue attaching the evergreen bundles all the way down the twine

until you reach the end, filling in the length and sides until it is as full as you'd like it.

8. Now cut the wire.
9. Use the floral wire to attach the dried pomegranates, magnolia leaves, and/or mercury ornaments to your taste.

THE LEGEND OF THE CLADDAGH RING

Once, long ago, on the west coast of Ireland, outside the walls of Galway, there rested a mystical fishing village called Claddagh. In that ocean-thrashed land on Galway Bay, a man named Richard Joyce was engaged to the love of his life. One week from his wedding day, pirates engulfed the peaceful village and Richard was kidnapped. On the high seas, mourning for his homeland and his fiancé, Richard Joyce was eventually sold to a Turkish goldsmith. For years he was alienated from his love in a faraway land, and there he learned the goldsmith trade. Never forgetting the woman he was forced to leave in the village, Richard designed the Claddagh ring — a circle of heart, crown, and hands, representing love, loyalty, and friendship — for the love he missed and ached for all his forlorn days.

Finally, after years of labor, Richard earned his freedom and returned to the

Claddagh Village to present his love with the ring and with his heart. She in turn had never given up and had waited for Richard. They vowed to never be separated again.

The ring he designed has come to represent not only the misty and mythical land of Ireland, but also the treasure that true love is to all who are willing to wait and all those who strive to return home.

Tradition tells us the following:

Worn on the right hand, crown turned inward, your heart is open. Worn on the right hand, crown turned outward, indicates a commitment to another. Worn on the left hand, crown turned outward, lets the world know two hearts have been bound together and that love and friendship together will reign forever, never to be separated.

THE STORY BEHIND
THE STORY

Dear Reader,

I have long been fascinated with the power of mythology and story to move and change the deeper aspects of ourselves. The myth of the Claddagh ring is one of my favorites — it is about the vulnerable strength of undying loyalty, friendship, and love. Combining mythology with songwriting and music is more fun than a writer should be allowed to have. In this story, both the music and the myth unite to bring Charlotte and Jimmy to a new place in their lives.

These characters have lived with me for a long while now. Every Christmas season we can find ourselves asking what is most important, *who* is most important. We can get lost in the chaos, the frivolity, and even the beauty of the season. But what happens when our hearts quiet? What opens up when our souls reach for what lasts?

I hope this story allows you to answer those questions for yourself.

With love,
Patti Callahan Henry

DISCUSSION QUESTIONS

1. What do you think of the title *The Perfect Love Song*? Do you think such a song can exist?

2. In this story, the song that was so "perfect" had a negative effect on Jimmy's life. Have you ever had something "perfect" come into your life, only to understand the negative influence it has on you or your loved ones?

3. Chapter 1 begins with the traditional Irish storyteller's opening, "May stillness be upon your thoughts and silence upon your tongue! For I tell you a tale that was told at the beginning . . . the one story worth telling . . ." The Irish have a rich cultural history of storytelling and of myths passed down from generation to generation much the way Maeve tells Kara her love story. Are all stories interconnected in some way? Do you think many modern stories are actually based on far

more ancient tales and myths? And if so, what are some examples?

4. Callahan Henry's fiction is a celebration of Southern Lowcountry culture and customs. You can often feel a novel's setting through the actual words used in telling the tale, the beauty in the language as it captures the spirit or energy of the characters or the smell of the sea and salty air. What is unique about the setting of this book, and how did it enhance the story? How much do you feel that the narrative voice is both affected and informed by place? And how does the use of sea imagery like the small shell Charlotte brings with her to the church in Ireland play into the narrative?

5. How do chance and destiny affect the characters in the novel as they make decisions and live and love? Are larger forces at work? Can we affect our fate?

6. The author writes about complex characters finding their place in the world, of the love and heartache in friendship, and of family and home. How do characters change or evolve throughout the course of the story? What events trigger such changes? Where do you see these characters in six months?

7. Jimmy and Jack had very difficult child-

hoods, and we learn that they were in fact abused by their alcoholic father. How does the past imprint their present-day lives and hinder their futures? Are they ever able to escape the effects of the past, and, if so, by what means?

8. When Jimmy tells Jack he will miss the wedding ceremony, Jack remarks "That's just great. Jimmy, always in time for the party." How does the concept of responsibility toward family play into the novel? Weddings are often a time of joy but also of incredible stress for families. What do you think it is about weddings in particular that can bring families closer together, or tear them apart?

9. The Claddagh ring appears throughout the novel. What is it about the ring that symbolizes the themes of love returning, reconciliation, and rebirth? How does this play into Jimmy's conversation with his father? How does Jimmy's need for his father's approval and his reunion with his father influence Jimmy to return to Charlotte's side?

10. The story outcome is greatly influenced by Maeve Mahoney, her stories and her advice. Do you believe that those who have passed on influence our lives and choices? If so, how?

11. Music is an important theme throughout the novel. Music becomes a father to Jimmy and Jack when their father is not in their lives and in turn, their band also becomes their family. How does involving yourself in art or music help to fill the void of a close personal relationship that is now lost? Do you think that music and art can be viable replacements for lost love? Or are music and art outlets for grief and loss?

12. The holiday season features prominently in *The Perfect Love Song,* and it is Christmas that brings everyone back together in the end. How do you give back during the holiday season? And are there ways that we can inspire others to remember to visit the elderly in our communities and to truly understand that giving is a gift in and of itself?

ABOUT THE AUTHOR

Patti Callahan Henry is a *New York Times* bestselling author. Patti was a finalist in the Townsend Prize for Fiction, has been an Indie Next Pick, twice an OKRA pick, and a multiple nominee for the Southern Independent Booksellers Alliance (SIBA) Novel of the Year. Her work has also been included in short story collections, anthologies, magazines and blogs. Patti attended Auburn University for her undergraduate work, and Georgia State University for her graduate degree. Once a Pediatric Clinical Nurse Specialist, she now writes full time. The mother of three children, she lives in both Mountain Brook, Alabama, and Bluffton, South Carolina, with her husband.

The employees of Thorndike Press hope you have enjoyed this Large Print book. All our Thorndike, Wheeler, and Kennebec Large Print titles are designed for easy reading, and all our books are made to last. Other Thorndike Press Large Print books are available at your library, through selected bookstores, or directly from us.

For information about titles, please call:
(800) 223-1244

or visit our website at:
gale.com/thorndike

To share your comments, please write:
Publisher
Thorndike Press
10 Water St., Suite 310
Waterville, ME 04901